MOUNTAIN MC

SNOW'S WOMAN

HALLIE BENNETT

SNOW'S WOMAN

REAPER'S WOLVES MOUNTAIN MC #1

HALLIE BENNETT

Searching for more mountain men? Check out the introduction to Suitor's Crossing and heart sparks in the Mountain Men of Suitor's Crossing series <u>here</u>[1]!

CHAPTER ONE

CAROLINE

I'm going to a real-life biker bar.

If this stupid shirt cooperates...

Tugging at the hem of my *Property of Flame* tee, my nerves become more frazzled. The thin fabric bunches around my thick waist, conforming to a couple of rolls, while the subtle stretching of fibers shows around my chest.

"Dammit."

I knew I should've gone a size up since it's women's sizing. We all know that shit ain't uniform—no matter where you go—but I was hoping a 3XL would do the job. Unfortunately, all it's "doing" is making me feel like a stuffed sausage, which is a shame because I love this shirt.

To celebrate the new release from one of our favorite authors, my romance book club is going to an actual biker bar, and we agreed to wear t-shirts showing support for our fictional MC boyfriends.

Which may be the wildest, most ridiculous thing I ever do, but Kat had the grand idea of experiencing "book life" in reality.

The four of us in the club—me, Kat, Amelie, and Beth—connected over our mutual love of alpha bikers and the obsessive love they have for their women a couple of years

1

ago. But, hopefully, we don't experience too much of a real motorcycle club's life tonight.

A fictional badass who falls hard for his girl? Yes, please!

But a potentially dangerous man who deals in drugs and violence? Hard pass.

Taking one last look in the mirror, I gather my courage and head outside, where Kat's laying on the car horn, praying we have a fun but uneventful night. Bars have never been my scene, but add hot, leather-clad bikers into the mix, and my anxiety's already shooting through the roof.

God, I hope I don't sweat through this shirt.

"Hey, girl, hop in!" Kat waits for me to settle into the passenger seat of her gold Camry before zipping out of the gravel parking area. She gets on the interstate, heading toward the mountains, as the robotic voice of her GPS says we'll arrive at our destination in an hour.

The four of us catch up on our day before switching to carpool karaoke, belting out our favorite songs until Amelie leans forward from the backseat.

"How did you find this place again?" she asks, and I turn down the energetic beat of Kat's pre-game playlist so we can hear her answer.

"It wasn't that difficult. These guys drive around town all the time. It was only a matter of following them."

Only Kat would think that was a logical thing to do.

She's the most outgoing in the club, which isn't saying much considering how shy and introverted the rest of us are, and she never fails to amaze us with her outrageous antics.

"Because that's perfectly reasonable," Beth adds from her place in the back with Amelie.

We laugh because, for Kat, it's true.

"You're lucky they didn't realize you were tailing them." I imagine some hulking biker pulling over to the side of the road and calling his buddies for backup because an unidentified vehicle is following him.

Sounds like the perfect start to an MC romance, actually...

"It's not like anything would've happened," Kat scoffs, exiting the interstate for an empty road leading into darkness.

Sometimes I forget how close we live to the wild in Everton. It's a decently sized city, but step outside its bounds and you're in the middle of nowhere. Pitch-black nothingness due to the absence of city lights.

"Can't say the same for us right now. Are you sure this is the right way? This looks sketchy as hell."

Pebbles crunch under the tires as we cautiously continue down another deserted road after the GPS tells Kat to turn left. A forest of trees surrounds us. Ducking my head, I peer out the window to look at the sky, but the treetops are too dense to find the moon or stars.

"Relax. It's a biker bar, not a McDonald's. They have to be secluded or else risk trouble." Kat's hands clench around the steering wheel. Despite her reassurance, it doesn't look like she's feeling as comfortable as she's acting.

"*Trouble.* You mean with cops? Jesus, Kat, where the hell are you taking us? We read about MCs because we don't actually want to get involved with them. The point is to keep a safe distance!" Always cautious, Beth's hands grip either side of mine and Kat's seats. "And this feels a long way from safe."

"I doubt an axe murderer's roaming around waiting to chop you up, Beth."

"No, just an entire motorcycle club intent on keeping their secrets private from obvious outsiders."

Neon lights blink through overgrown branches, and a swarm of fearful little bees buzzes to life in my gut.

Oh my god, we're here.

We're actually doing this.

Lines of motorcycles guard the front of a dissolute wooden building like a steel horse barricade. Men and women lounge against the bikes and each other, beer bottles in one hand while the other's busy holding their partner.

"Too late to back out now." Kat parks the car, drawing a couple of curious stares, and we file out like prisoners on execution row.

Swallowing the metallic taste of worry in my mouth, I let Kat lead as the rest of us timidly followed her into the smoky bar. Thankfully, there's an empty table near the center of the bar that we snag, plopping into the rickety chairs with relief.

"Now, that we're here... What are we supposed to do?"

It feels like everyone's staring at us, wondering why the hell we wandered in here. As someone who's used to being in the background, it's an unnerving sensation.

I don't like being the center of attention, especially when it's because I don't fit in. Years of sitting alone in the school cafeteria rise up to bathe me in self-conscious insignificance.

"Drink." Shedding her jacket, Kat reveals her *Property of Styx* tee and heads toward the bar, returning minutes later with a tray of shots. "Bottoms up!"

Beth declines a shot glass since she's the designated driver. Reassured that someone will be keeping an eye on us tonight, I down the tequila—the burning warmth immediately working to calm me.

Maybe tonight won't be so bad.

Maybe it'll be one of those things where you hesitate to accept the event invitation, but in the end, it's worth attending.

I survey the room, noting the faded pictures and signs hanging on the walls. It's not as crowded as I expected for a Saturday night.

Men fill the space, with a few sparsely dressed women sitting on their laps. In fact, our little group seems to be the only one not looking to hook up.

Are these women considered biker bunnies? Is that a thing?

Everyone laughs. "Why don't you ask, Caro?"

Guess I thought out loud.

"No, thanks," I mutter.

Nothing wrong with being a biker bunny if that's what you want, but I sure as hell don't have the confidence to be one. Or to talk with one, no matter how interested I am in learning about their lives. To see how much of what I read emulates real life.

Probably zero.

I'm about two shots and a bottle of water in when my body reminds me that I'm a thirty-one-year-old woman and not some co-ed meant to drink all night without consequences.

Bouncing my knee under the table, I scan the bar for a restroom when a dim sign in the back catches my eye.

Thank god.

"I'll be right back."

The bathroom isn't in the best of shape, and there's a short line, but at least it does the job. Grateful for not ending up peeing in the woods, I wash my hands and retrace my steps when a tattooed hulk intercepts me.

A head taller than me with broad shoulders, his inked arms cross over the firm muscles of his chest as he glares at me. "You know, it's pretty fucking stupid for an encroaching club to let its women out alone on the home club's turf."

It takes me a minute to sort through his words. Encroaching club? Home turf?

"Yeah, I guess so. Excuse me." I try to go around him, thinking he has the wrong girl, but he steps to the side, blocking me.

"Then why the fuck are you here? Is this a subtle power play?" The man moves closer, the smell of leather and motor oil coming off him.

That should not be as intoxicating as it is.

Puts my poor Mahogany Woods candle scent to shame.

"I'm sorry, but I have no idea what you're talking about. Will you please let me pass?"

He raises his hand and draws a finger down my chest, sending chills down my spine—whether in fear or lust, I don't know. But a man's never touched me that way, or ever, since I'm a freaking virgin, and however inappropriate, the brief touch is definitely eliciting a fluttery reaction.

"Property of Flame. Hades Hangmen. Your man. His club." His growled words penetrate my fog.

"Wait. You think I'm in an MC?" I laugh in surprise.

How a girl like me could possibly be mistaken for a club member is beyond me. But I suppose in his life, it's smart to be wary of unknown people and potential threats. Not that I've ever been categorized as a threat.

Short, curvy, and responsible.

Those are my categories.

Every teacher in grade school wrote "conscientious" on my report card, and I've never veered off the path of being good or doing what's right. The closest I've gotten are the books I've read. Stories about brave heroines who own their sexuality, take risks, and fall in love with bad boys.

Like this giant biker who's staring bullet holes through me.

"I think your man is." Confusion finally seeps into his gray gaze, but the hard tone doesn't leave his voice.

"I don't have a man," I stupidly admit. I'm not sure if it's the smartest thing to say, considering my predicament, but it's got to be better than him thinking we're from a rival club about to start a turf war.

"Who's Flame? You're wearing his fucking name across your tits."

Whoa...

If I were another girl in an alternate reality, I might detect a note of jealousy in his grumbly tone, but that's impossible. You don't get to be a thirty-one-year-old virgin because men flock to you—or become jealous of your imaginary book boyfriend.

"He's a character in a book. My friends and I have a book club, and we're celebrating a new release in our favorite series about an MC. It's all fictional. There is no Flame. He doesn't exist."

Of all the ways I saw this night playing out, being mistaken for a fictional MC member's "old lady" never factored in.

His body loses some of its rigidity at my explanation, and I exhale a breath of relief. Good, he believes me.

"Am I free to go now?"

A second passes like a weak internet connection trying to load until he backs off, letting me pass without a word.

Instantly, I race toward the safety of my friends, fidgeting with the flimsy fabric of my shirt. Sweat causes the cotton to cling to my skin even more, and I pray there aren't dark marks on my back or under my arms from overheating.

Physically broadcasting how worked-up he made me would be humiliating.

"What took you so long?" Amelie asks once I slide into my seat and chug the last of my water.

After sharing the debacle, they immediately start searching the bar for the stranger.

"Holy shit! He's fucking hot! You are so lucky." Kat fans herself.

"I wouldn't call it luck." I sneak another peek at the Tattooed Hulk.

He's sitting at the bar with a few other men. They all wear the same patch on their backs: Reaper's Wolves. An intense wolf's mouth is open wide, ready to tear anyone to pieces, and a shudder of realization shakes me to the core.

I talked to an actual MC member.

Damn.

No matter what books I like, it's all fantasy.

Real-life MCs?

You don't mess with them.

CHAPTER TWO

SNOW

Her group tries to inconspicuously study me as I take a drink.

A bunch of curious good girls here for a little excitement—I noticed them right away. In a room full of predators, sweet prey is always easy to spot. And, damn, did they look sweet.

Especially *her*—the curvy little package with wild curls and innocent blue eyes behind square-framed glasses.

But when I saw what she was wearing, fury ran through me. What man lets his woman into the lion's den without protection? Let her blatantly flaunt his MC in rival territory?

When she explained how they were here because of a book, relief washed through me. Then, frustration. Innocent women like her don't belong here.

"I think you've wet all of their panties, Prez. They won't stop spying." Fox, my vice president, laughs and relaxes on the bar stool next to mine.

"Let's hope they look their fill and get the hell out of here. Where are we with Breaker?"

The only reason we're in this dive bar is to negotiate a deal with the local chapter of the Ghost Rider MC. They run the territory from Everton to the county line.

Since my club's arrival in Suitor's Crossing two years ago, we've staved off our fair share of challenges from groups concerned about our intentions. This is just another one to add to the list.

The Reaper's Wolves MC is home to ex-military men searching for brotherhood. We're above board and try to keep to ourselves, but that doesn't mean we don't respond to threats.

Tonight, we're trying to broker peace with the Ghost Rider MC and defuse the tension between our clubs.

They want to do illegal shit? Fine, but we don't want any part of it. And we're sure as hell not planning on stealing their business.

"He and his boys are late, of course. An immature power play." Fox rolls his eyes.

"I'm tired of dealing with these pissants. We don't start shit yet still have to parlay with insecure men." I shake my head in disgust. "Is it too much to ask to leave us the fuck alone? We just want some peace after the hell we've all been through."

"I hear ya, brother."

My dad founded the Reaper's Wolves after serving during the Gulf War. My earliest memories are of the rumble of Harleys and men's laughter as they gathered at their home away from home—my family's ranch house.

I always knew I wanted to follow in Dad's footsteps, but damn, I don't remember him being forced to handle rival clubs' feelings.

Not that I truly consider any of these MCs rivals.

We're not in the same business, after all, but there's a fine line between showing your strength to ward off problems and laying low and leaving yourself open to being run over.

Stretching my neck from side to side, I force the muscles to loosen from pent-up tension. I hate being kept waiting. And I hate that we're in No Man's Land, a neutral space for clubs to meet in safety.

My best friend Austin's bar is home. So is the small mountain town of Suitor's Crossing.

Those winding mountain roads are calling my name, but there's another beacon drawing my attention, too—the curvy good girl I can't keep my eyes off of.

Despite No Man's Land's neutrality, anything can happen to a woman like her and her friends. This area may not officially be owned by any one club, but I'd hoped a warning about encroaching clubs and rival turf might send her little group running for the hills.

Because they don't belong here.

Yet their sense of self-preservation is clearly lacking because they still remain front and center in the bar. On display for every hardened biker with a criminal record or strung-out tweaker to harass.

"Make sure we've got men watching them." I nod toward her group.

Fox smirks but agrees.

Who knows what will go down when the Ghost Rider MC arrives? But we don't want civilians accidentally getting caught in the crossfire.

Just as the words leave my mouth, the Little Owl heads my way.

Her glasses accentuate the air of innocence about her when she adjusts them, and the serene blue draws me in like she's a fucking mermaid of the sea. She pushes a stray curl behind her ear—one that refuses to be tamed because it pops forward again—before ordering another round of shots.

"On me, Lou." I motion to the bartender as he pours the alcohol. I shouldn't prolong her stay in No Man's Land, but it's a bad habit—buying pretty girls drinks.

"No, thank you." She dips her chin in acknowledgment and puts cash on the countertop. Short fingernails tap against the bartop as she shifts from one foot to the other.

"Accept it as an apology for earlier."

Lou pushes the tray of shots toward her, the golden liquor gleaming under the bar lights, but again, she quietly refuses and walks away.

Fox snickers at her rejection as I swallow the last of my beer.

I'm the fucking president of Reaper's Wolves.

I don't get turned down.

Women flock to my side for a chance at the MC president, and a shared drink hardly counts as a commitment.

Logic wars with pride.

It's smart to decline my offer. She doesn't know me except as the man who cornered and interrogated her—a stranger in a potentially dangerous place.

Doesn't lessen the sting of her rebuff, though.

Not one fucking bit.

CHAPTER THREE

CAROLINE

My phone rings as we prepare to leave an hour later. "Just a second, it's my cousin."

I don't know why she's calling me at this time of night. Lauren started texting something about an emergency after my encounter with the Tattooed Hulk, but I learned long ago that she exaggerates everything.

Answering the call, I walk outside, where it's quieter. "Hey, what's going on?"

"What? I can't want to talk to my favorite cousin?"

"At midnight? No." I know I'm being rude, but this is just like her. Lauren and I grew up together—more like sisters than cousins—but we've never meshed very well.

"God, relax. We haven't talked in forever. I wanted to see how you were since you never call me."

There's a reason for that.

Closing my eyes in frustration, I lean against the building. "I'm fine. How's Matt?"

Lauren latches onto the subject and proceeds to tell me every detail of their idyllic lives. Matt and Lauren married after three months of dating. I've only met him once, and it wasn't at their elopement, which I didn't attend.

That's our kind of dysfunctional relationship.

Someone leaves the bar to the left of me, and a click precedes the appearance of a flame. The man stands in the shadows, smoke the only indication that someone's there.

My body tenses, the hair rising on the back of my neck. It occurs to me how dumb it is to be out here alone—even if my friends *are* inside.

A few couples remain scattered around the parking lot, but they're focused on each other. Not me and whoever this stranger is.

Trying to act casual, I push off the wall and amble toward the entrance. Lauren is still talking, so at least she'll hear me scream if something happens.

But before I even walk two steps, the stranger cages me against the wall, and my phone clatters to the ground at the sudden movement. I tell myself to scream, but nothing comes out.

I'm frozen.

All that registers is the familiar scent of smoke and oil. Glancing upward, I recognize the man from inside—the Tattooed Hulk.

"You embarrassed me in there." His rough voice comes out low and dangerous.

Shit, I should've accepted his drink offer. But all I could think was that I'd owe him. That he'd feel entitled to something he wasn't.

You really need to stop overthinking situations.

"If you were a man, you would've been flat on your back after defying me."

"If I were a man, I don't think you would've bought me a drink."

He jerks in surprise at my comeback.

Keep your mouth shut, Caroline. Don't antagonize him!

A flash of amusement crosses his expression before settling into an intimidating scowl.

Did I imagine the brief softening?

"Maybe getting you on your back shouldn't be counted out yet."

My breath picks up at his suggestion. A thrill of excitement spikes in my blood as anxiety and—*lust?*—build beneath my skin.

"Try it and see what happens," I dare. I've never dared a man in my life, but my crazy ass decides this is the one to challenge. The alcohol must be screwing with my good sense.

He drives a large hand through the waves of his brown hair and huffs in frustration. The disheveled look suits him, along with his trimmed beard. And the stack of muscles bunching under his tee. And those tattoos...

Stop staring!

"Don't tempt me, Little Owl."

The pet name confuses me, but he continues, "Tonight I'm feeling generous since you obviously had no idea what you were walking into. But don't make the same mistake twice. Because if I see you or any of your little friends here again, there *will* be consequences. Got it?"

I nod. God knows what his consequences will be.

Getting you on your back, duh!

The thought really shouldn't encourage me to return and find out.

"Hey, Snow, when you're done with the girl, we've got business to take care of. Our guests are here."

I jump at the interruption, but Snow doesn't respond, just watches me. When he's satisfied with whatever he's searching for, he retreats with a wave of his arm.

"After you."

I hurry in front of him to get inside, and his heat on my back lets me know he's not far behind. Once I reach our table, I don't bother to sit.

"Let's go. We need to leave."

"Why? What happened?"

"Just trust me. Come on." Snagging my purse, I urge them up and out. As soon as we've left the parking lot, I explain what happened, and shocked silence fills the car.

"Holy fuck!" Kat bursts out.

Yep, that sounds about right.

CHAPTER FOUR

SNOW

"Finished putting the fear of God in her?" Fox asks.

"She won't be back." I ignore a pulse of regret—which makes no fucking sense—and follow Fox to the back of the bar, where the Ghost Rider MC president and his VP wait in a corner booth.

Our respective club members stand guard, hands crossed at their waists, hooded eyes studying each other's movements for potential threats.

"Nice of you to join us." I slip into the booth and try to focus on the men in front of me rather than the woman I just ran out of here.

Her little book club is swiftly heading out the bar exit, and I'm relieved she finally took my warnings to heart.

The weight on my chest dissolves, allowing my lungs to drag in a calming breath now that I know the Little Owl is safely out of harm's way.

"So, you're the Reaper's Wolves President." It's not a question. Breaker, the Ghost Rider President, hunches over the table. "Heard you were a big motherfucker."

Rolling my shoulders, I study him just as thoroughly. He looks like most of the guys in my crew—bulky with muscle and hardened by life. "And I heard you're concerned with our presence in the area."

"Can you blame me? Another club shows up out of the blue; it's my job to ensure my club's assets are protected."

My jaw clenches at his insinuation. "We haven't touched your assets and don't plan to. Can you say the same? Our strip club on Byron Street has had a string of break-ins lately."

Which is what prompted this meeting in the first place.

Despite our security, the perps managed to bypass the alarms and rob the club while proudly wearing their Ghost Rider cuts. I want it to stop, and I want to know who the fuck fed them the security information.

Breaker shrugs, noncommittal. "That's a shame, but we weren't involved with anything. Sounds like you might need to report your little problem to the cops."

Knowing smirks and snickers erupt at the suggestion. It's no secret that the local law enforcement around here is shady as fuck.

Sheriff Lawson in Suitor's Crossing is a good man, as are his deputies. But Everton PD? Not so much.

"I'd prefer to keep the cops out of our business, wouldn't you?"

"Now that's something we can both agree on. Listen, I'm not opposed to a peace treaty between our clubs. Frankly, we've got more important issues to deal with than your little recreational club. Though it's always good to know where you stand with each other, right?"

I agree with a stiff nod.

"Excellent. Then what do you say we call a truce?" Breaker offers his hand across the table.

I make him wait, his hand hovering in the air, before accepting it. In my mind, it wasn't much of a truce when we never entered his game of breaking and entering, but if that's what he wants to call it, fine.

As long as they leave us the fuck alone.

We've got a couple of strip clubs and other business ventures in Everton, High Ridge, and Suitor's Crossing that keep our club flush with cash without needing to resort to selling drugs or weapons like the Ghost Rider MC. They can keep that shit on their side of town while we do our thing.

Legitimate business, free of trouble.

Mostly.

We still have issues with assholes challenging us at the Ole Aces bar, and Austin's about ready to start charging the club for all the damage our prospects incur when they give in to the local taunting.

However, bar fights are a far cry from running drugs across county or state lines.

Years ago, we swore oaths to our country, and while none of us serve anymore, we still consider it our duty to protect and serve the people around us. That doesn't include providing addicts with cocaine or adding more weapons to the streets.

Once we conclude our business with Breaker and his club, Fox and I head out along with the rest of our men. It's late, and I'm ready to crash for the night.

Maybe I'll even dream about my Little Owl...

Because I doubt we'll ever run into each other again.

CHAPTER FIVE

CAROLINE

Big block letters declare "FREE AIR" at the edge of the gas station parking lot, and I angle toward an empty parking space in front of the metal machine.

Ever since my aunt died from her tire blowing out on the highway, I've been paranoid about checking the pressure before any trip longer than twenty minutes. Afraid something will happen while I'm driving seventy miles an hour and unable to react in time.

Thanks, anxiety and intrusive thoughts.

Grabbing my tire gauge from the glove compartment, I step out and start unwinding the black hose when a familiar roar sounds behind me.

I swear, motorcycles are everywhere now. Kat wasn't kidding when she said there were tons in town, but I guess I never really noticed until MCs became more real than fantasy.

Until a tattooed biker president entered my life.

Forget him and that ill-conceived night.

But it's difficult when all those romances I've read meld into hot dreams where he's the leading man.

"As if you would ever feel comfortable enough to do even half the things in those dreams," I mutter to myself.

Kneeling at the front of my car, I unscrew the knob covering the tire opening and pop my gauge in with a defeated sigh. I wouldn't know the first thing about fitting into a biker's life.

The little barometer pops out on the tire gauge. *Twenty-eight.* That's a long way from where it should be at thirty-six.

I punch the needed pressure amount into the machine before bringing the end of the hose closer to the first tire, the rubbery tubing flouncing around like an agitated snake.

Squeezing the odd handle in my hand, I try to figure out how it works. All the machines I've used in the past just started when I connected the parts, but nothing seems to happen when I press these two together.

Just my luck.

"Need help?" The amused question rumbles from over my head, and I glance up to see someone silhouetted against the sun.

Great, I have a witness to my ignorance. Stalling, I stick the tire gauge back in the socket to see if anything's changed.

Maybe air was passing through the hose, but it was too quiet for me to hear?

"You did that already." The stranger squats beside me, and I recognize the man from the bar two weeks ago—Snow, the Reaper's Wolves MC President.

He commandeers the hose from my lax grip, places it in position, and pulls the handle. "You have to hold this down for it to fill up; otherwise, you're decreasing the pressure."

Geez, they need instructions displayed to help a girl out.

"I would've figured it out," I defend myself before pausing and adding, "But thanks."

No need to be a bitch to this guy, even though he did scare the hell out of me that night.

And turn you on.

And feature in more than a few nights' worth of sexy dreams.

"You're welcome." He hands the hose back to me so I can try. Now that he's shown me, it seems obvious.

Shaking my head at the blonde moment, I move on to the back tires. He doesn't say anything else; he just watches me, and his blatant stare sends a wave of nerves surging through me.

What does he want?

"I'll be done soon," I say, praying for the airflow to quicken its pace in case he needs to use the machine, too.

"Take your time. I'm waiting for my tank to fill up."

My eyebrows raise. "It's probably full by now."

He shrugs but doesn't leave.

Okay... Cue more nerves.

When the machine emits a repetitive beeping sound, I double-check the numbers before coiling the cord again and fighting the twisting hose. Sirens wail down the street, making their way toward us as I finish.

Raising my voice, I say, "Thanks for—"

The words have barely left my mouth when the screeching squeal of tires transforms into a booming crash, and my body slams into Snow's—both of us thrown to the ground.

A cloud of smoke and glass obscures the gas station as I dazedly roll off the firm body beneath me and search for my fallen glasses on the asphalt. Disjointed car alarms pierce the air, and my mind struggles to figure out what happened.

"Are you okay?" Snow gently fits my glasses over the bridge of my nose and ears. His large hands push my hair out of my face as his concerned eyes meet mine.

Taking a deep breath to calm down, I choke out, "I think so," before spasming into a coughing fit.

My body's shaking; adrenaline is coursing through my veins. A loud ringing pulses in my ears when I see my car slammed into the air pump with another vehicle behind it.

There's a cop car and a red Corvette at the center of a collision in front of the gas station. It looks like they set off a chain of events that ended with my car being smashed by a rogue Taurus.

A man stumbles out of the car, holding one of his arms to his chest, while a streak of blood falls from a cut on his temple.

"Jesus," I whisper before Snow tucks my head into his chest and holds me when another coughing fit wracks my lungs. His strong arms form a brief safe haven before we're interrupted by an officer emerging from the smoke.

"Sir, I'm Sergeant Benton; are you and the lady alright?" He addresses Snow, which is fine by me since I'm struggling to speak without erupting into a spat of coughs. Besides, only one thought blazes loud and clear in my otherwise muddled brain: I could've died.

If I'd been on the other side of my car... If I'd still been kneeling on the ground... Who knows what damage could've been done?

"She needs to be checked out by an EMT... Maybe taken to the hospital."

Snow's low suggestion snaps me out of my fog. "No, I'm fine. No hospital."

"Are you sure, ma'am?"

I nod my aching head, ignoring its throbbing. An exorbitant hospital bill won't fit into my limited budget, especially now that I have to contend with a totaled car.

Wasn't I attempting to avoid an accident by ensuring my tires were at the correct pressure? Talk about life's cruel sense of humor.

Snow wraps an arm around my waist and helps me stand on wobbly legs. I lean heavily on him, afraid of falling. It's an odd sensation—feeling every pinpoint of atoms zing into chaos while also experiencing weightlessness as if I'll float away if Snow isn't here to ground me.

An hour later, after talking to the police and my insurance company, I sign an AMA form—each task becoming heavier as the adrenaline in my blood slowly fades.

Snow hasn't left my side, and while logically I know I should keep my distance, the majority of me is grateful to have his support. Whenever I falter, he steps in, and it's nice to let someone else lead for once.

After receiving the okay to leave, I approached my crumpled car in trepidation. What am I going to do? The insurance guy said it can take anywhere from a few days to a couple of weeks before they reimburse me for a new car, which means I'm screwed until then.

My mint green purse peeks out from beneath the crush of glass and metal, and a wave of relief hits me at its appearance. At least I've still got my license and bank cards readily available.

Except a tattooed hand stops me from reaching into the vehicle.

"Oh no, you don't. I'll get whatever you need. I don't want you getting any more cuts." Snow braces a hand on the outer frame as he leans in and catches the purse strap. The white bandage around his forearm covers the few scrapes he sustained in the accident.

"But it's alright if you do?"

"Yes."

One word, and my knees threaten to buckle again because it's endearing how serious he is about protecting me. Even from this small thing.

Flushing under his penetrating gaze, I duck my head and rifle through my purse for a distraction. The cool casing of my phone brushes my hand, and I latch onto a new topic. "Hopefully, my phone's okay since I need to call someone to pick me up."

"Don't bother. You're riding with me."

"That's not necessary..." My protest is cut off as he guides me toward two bikes, where a tall man leans against one, observing the scene. A scattered crowd of people stared at the wreckage behind us.

"Y'all good to go?" the stranger asks, remarkably calm considering the circumstances. Snow nods, then pats the backseat of his motorcycle.

I should refuse his offer again, but at this point, fatigue is wearing on me, so I rattle off my address instead.

What's another twenty minutes with him anyway? It's better than hanging out here waiting for a friend to pick me up.

"Do you have another helmet?" A thought for safety flits through my mind.

I've never ridden on a motorcycle, and the idea that soon I'll know what it's like to have hundreds of pounds of metal vibrating between my legs leaves me cautiously thrilled. Too bad I'm probably concussed and can't properly enjoy it.

"Do you think I'd let you ride unprotected?"

I remain silent.

I don't know him or what he's like—except for the fact that he's president of a motorcycle club, warned me away from him the last time we spoke, and has the most piercing silver eyes I've ever seen.

Hmm... I guess I know three things.

He lifts an extra helmet from a compartment on the back of the bike and fastens it over my head, carefully jostling it around as he double-checks the fit. Grunting in satisfaction, Snow gestures for me to follow after he climbs onto the bike.

"Hold tight, and if you need me to stop, tap my shoulder. Okay?"

Giving him a thumbs up, I rest my head against his back and lock my arms around his firm waist. This could be a fantasy borne of my excessive reading habit—the hot biker from my past comes to rescue me from danger, whisking me away on his steel horse.

But it's all too real when the growl of his bike flares to life, and my headache intensifies because of it.

This isn't a romance novel.

Snow's not obsessed with me.

He's not a knight in shining armor who's fallen for the damsel in distress.

He's just a man looking out for a woman after sharing a traumatic experience together.

Soon, I'll be home, Snow will return to his life as an MC president, and we'll both forget about this strange interlude. It's for the best, but my body's chemical balance must still be off-kilter because the realization fills me with sadness and regret.

If only I were a different sort of girl...

The kind who dared to flirt with her rescuer or leap into his mysterious life without fear. The kind who, at the end of this bike ride, would thank him with a kiss or give him her number, or do just about anything else except for what I plan on doing—expressing my gratitude and then high-tailing it to the safety of my home without a backward glance.

Because I understand reality.

I'm a thirty-one-year-old virgin with curves to spare who's "conscientious" and never makes a move without agonizing over the decision.

And Snow?

Well, besides being a giant tattooed biker who has me dreaming of breaking the rules, he's already told me I don't belong in his world.

And I plan on listening to him.

CHAPTER SIX

SNOW

Timber and I arrive at the clubhouse an hour after leaving the gas station.

What a nightmare that turned into!

We'd been in Everton to check on the latest security installment at our club on Byron Street since wrapping up the deal with Breaker. What should've been a quick fill-up before hitting the road had morphed into a freak accident due to an asshole running a red light and driving straight into a cop speeding toward an incident.

The only positive thing to come out of the entire shitshow was running into my Little Owl again, or Caroline, as she'd told the officer.

I'm not sure what the odds are that we'd visit the same gas station at the same time, but it's got me wondering if there isn't something to Suitor's Crossing's myth about soulmates or *heart sparks*.

Despite it being a bad idea, I haven't been able to shake this girl from my head, and she's been whipping up unfamiliar emotions ever since our meeting. Saying we're soulmates may be far-fetched, but fate definitely seems to be at work here.

Killing the engine, I kick the stand down before carefully maneuvering off the bike, dislodging Little Owl's grip.

"Where are we? This isn't my apartment." She must've kept her eyes closed the entire time, or maybe that hit on her head was worse than she let on, because we'd been driving way longer than it would've taken to get to the address she gave me back in Everton.

Yet she never tapped my shoulder to have me pull over for questioning.

"You might have declined to see a doctor in Everton, but you're sure as hell gonna see one here."

She removes the bike helmet, and hundreds of wispy curls pop free. On instinct, my hand smooths over the amber chaos, rubbing the strands between my rough fingertips.

"Come on, Little Owl, let's get you checked out."

She warily eyes the two-story warehouse we converted into our clubhouse, complete with rooms for members and communal living spaces. It doesn't look like much from the outside, though—just a concrete building with windows.

"You've got a doctor here?"

"We've got a lot more than that, baby." I usher her inside the main living area as Saber, a former field surgeon for the army, rushes in with his bag of instruments.

"Timber said you were in an accident." Saber gestures to my arm, where it slid across the asphalt upon impact.

"I'm fine. An EMT cleaned and bandaged it. Look after her instead." Saber jerks to a stop until I glare at him and point to Caroline. "Her. First."

Shaking his head, he stoops in front of Little Owl. "Okay, follow my finger." He watches her for a moment before moving on to test her reflexes and hearing.

After a few more minutes, Saber concludes, "She definitely has a concussion."

"I figured as much," Caroline says, wilting in her chair at our resident poker table.

"It sucks, I know, but once we get you cleaned up, you'll feel a little better." He pulls an antibacterial wipe from his bag and moves to scrub the streak of ash on her cheek, but I've had enough. His official exam is over. He doesn't need to touch her again.

"Saber!"

Caroline jumps at my voice. Trying to reign in my possessiveness, I stride forward, placing a comforting hand on her shoulder.

"I'll take it from here."

"Whatever you say, boss, but if she's staying the night, you need to wake her every two hours to ensure nothing's wrong."

"Oh, I'm not..."

"Yes, you are." Of course, she's staying. My Little Owl was dropped into my lap like destiny herself had a hand in it. I'm not going to let this opportunity pass without getting to know Caroline better.

Leaning down, I scoop her into my arms, and despite her protests, she wraps her arms around me and snuggles into my neck like she belongs there.

Because she does.

I enter my private master suite down the hall and set her on the bathroom counter. Immediately, she leans her head against the mirror and closes her eyes.

"Hey." I gently tap her cheek. "Don't fall asleep yet, baby. Give me five minutes, then I'll let you rest."

Wetting a rag, I make quick work of cleaning her up, carefully removing her glasses to reveal her gorgeous eyes, unhindered except for her drooping lashes. While I'd like to take my time revealing her soft skin, my Little Owl is barely staying awake as it is.

"I'm Caroline, not *baby*," she drawls, her nose scrunching in an adorable expression of disapproval.

"And I'm Snow, but you *are* my baby. I let you go at the bar and warned you what would happen if I saw you again." Even though I didn't know my intentions then, I want her, and now fate's given me a hand in keeping her.

Caroline remains unconvinced with her wrinkled forehead and pursed lips, but she doesn't refute my comment.

"Hang on, let me get you something to sleep in." I grab a Reaper's Wolves tee from a drawer before returning to the bathroom. Soon she'll be wearing a *Property of Snow* shirt.

Fuck that Flame tee of hers.

Who cares if he's a fictional character? The only man's name to cover her body will be mine.

My hands start lifting her torn sweatshirt when she swats my hand away. "I can do it. Turn around."

Sighing, I follow orders, listening carefully for any problems before whipping back around two minutes later. "You need to lose the jeans, too."

A cute smirk twists her mouth as she knowingly wags her pointer finger in my face. "You didn't give me bottoms."

Damn, I'd hoped she wouldn't notice.

After Caroline's changed into a fresh tee and sweatpants, I hover behind her while she climbs into my bed and under the covers.

"I still don't understand why you brought me here. Your doctor's nice and all but wasn't necessary. You're lucky I'm too tired to argue, so I'm just gonna go with it." She yawns, lessening the impact of her annoyed resignation.

A grin twitches on my cheeks at her rambling, though I resist the urge to give in, not wanting to upset her when she needs rest.

"Good. You need someone looking after you tonight, and I'm your man." The declaration lodges firmly in my chest, like it's been waiting for me to admit the truth out loud.

"I could already have one at home. This could be considered kidnapping," she mumbles. Her head's on my pillow as she lays on her side to face me.

Balancing on the edge of the mattress, I lean over and cage her against the bed with my fists braced on either side of the pillow. Her breathing escalates as she arches her neck to look me in the eye, curiosity warring with confusion.

If she didn't have a concussion—and was fully aware of her situation—I'd lick a path from that extended tendon to her ear and whisper all the filthy things I wanted to do to her curvy little body before fucking her into the bed.

But she does have a concussion, so back off.

"You don't have a man, remember? That's what you told me at the bar."

"I could have a roommate."

"I thought you said you were too tired to argue," I whisper, tempted to kiss her good night until common sense kicks in and I retreat with a sigh. "I'll be back to check on you in a few hours, alright?"

A grumbled agreement is muffled by the covers as she closes her eyes.

Sleep has finally won the battle.

The backs of my fingers caress her round cheek for a brief moment, then I return to the bathroom for a quick shower. Peeling the gauze away from my arm reveals the wound's stopped bleeding—a minor scratch compared to Caroline's concussion.

I hate that I wasn't able to protect her from injury earlier, but it's my mission to ensure her safety in the future.

Slipping on a pair of gray sweatpants, I ease into bed next to my Little Owl after setting an alarm for two hours from now. Saber said she needs to be monitored while sleeping, and that's exactly what I'm going to do.

Concussion be damned.

Nothing's going to steal my Little Owl away now.

CHAPTER SEVEN

SNOW

A chill wakes me the next morning. Caroline's curled on the opposite side of the bed—cocooned in most of the blankets—with her back turned to me, so all I see are her curls spanning the distance between us.

A distance I'm irrationally pissed to see.

If she needed warmth, why didn't she stay cuddled by my side? Instead, even in sleep, her body kept walls around her.

Which is a radical change from the women I'm used to.

They throw themselves at me, eager to fuck the president of an MC and a military veteran to boot. Yet the woman I want is the complete opposite, leaving me to freeze my balls off despite having her warmth beside me.

Growling in frustration, I reach out to wake her, but when Caroline doesn't immediately respond, panic replaces my frustration and sends my heart racing. Maybe her injury was more severe than Saber thought.

My hand shakes her shoulder again.

"Caroline! Wake up, baby. Let me see those pretty blue eyes."

Finally, she rolls over and her lashes flutter open to reveal a bright azure clouded with sleep, and a sigh of relief escapes my chest, my lungs able to take a full breath again. It takes a second before her surroundings register, and then the clouds evaporate into recognition.

Frantic, she bolts to a sitting position before wincing in pain.

"Hey, take it easy. You have a concussion, remember?"

My hand covers hers where she gently cups the back of her head. I feel the raised bump, gently probing the knot as her curls tangle around my fingers.

"You slept in here?"

"It's my room, and you needed constant supervision." I don't add that there's no way in hell I'd be sleeping somewhere other than my bed, especially when she's in it.

An indefinable thread has drawn me to Caroline since the first time I saw her, despite my weak attempt to fight it. Resisting now, after the universe returned her to me, seems futile.

"Right..." She studies the comforter covering her legs, picking at the worn edge.

Maybe I should consider replacing the bed set as an unfamiliar rush of shame courses through me at its ragged state. Caroline deserves better than tattered bedspreads and lumpy pillows. Silk and satin should be the only fabrics allowed to stroke her supple curves.

"I should get going." Shoving the blanket away, she slides to the edge of the bed, tiptoes around a pair of haphazardly thrown socks and boots, then gathers the clothes she wore yesterday from the bathroom.

"Hang on. You can't wear those. They're torn and dirty from the accident." I open a few drawers and get her a new Reaper's Wolves tee and another pair of sweatpants.

Caroline pauses with the bathroom door halfway shut before swinging it open and exiting. "Good point. But I don't need another set of your clothes." She tugs on the tee she's wearing. "These are good enough to get me home."

"If that's what you want." Grabbing the back of my collar, I pull my worn shirt off instead.

Caroline's eyes go wide at the sight of my bare chest on display, and she quickly turns around, eliciting a low chuckle from me.

My innocent Little Owl.

"How about we find something to eat? You must be starving since we kind of skipped dinner last night."

Caroline nods as I finish changing and lead her downstairs to the kitchen, where we see one of the biker bunnies frying eggs.

Dammit.

Tiffany and I'd fucked a couple of times, but once she started acting like she had a right to me, I shut that shit down. I've been ignoring her for months to get the point across—no one owns me.

"Hey, honey."

Her syrupy greeting grates on my nerves as she sets a plate of scrambled eggs in front of me. I slide it toward Caroline, who's sitting next to me at the kitchen island, oblivious to the little snub.

There's a noticeable tightening in Tiffany's face as she scowls at my gesture. But she needs to learn real quick how things work around here, or she'll be out, because club whores are a dime a dozen.

"Thank you," Caro says gingerly. I don't know if it's for me or Tiffany, but I watch as she slowly eats and Tiffany cracks open more eggs.

Fox ambles through the kitchen door, dressed for the day in jeans and a black cutoff. He takes a place next to Caroline, and I hold back a growl at his closeness to her. Fox can be charming when he wants, but he damn well better know she's mine.

"How are you feeling?" Fox asks. He pours a cup of orange juice from the pitcher on the counter, chugging the full glass before pouring another.

"I've been better." Caroline smiles weakly before focusing on eating. She takes small, delicate bites... The kind I imagine giving her.

Forget it. She's nowhere near letting you touch her.

"You know... I read those books your little club likes to read."

That gets her attention. Caroline's head snaps up as she stares at Fox, a scarlet blush flooding her neck and cheeks.

"Yeah, lots of kinky fuckery going on in there. You're secretly a very naughty..."

"Fox!" I bark before he can finish his sentence. He's lucky Caroline's between us or else I'd punch the smug look off his face for even thinking about my woman that way.

Tiffany cuts in, "Who has time to read about fucking when you can experience the real thing? Only sad housewives read those kinds of books. Pathetic women who need softcore porn like *Fifty Shades* to get off."

She smirks, causing her artificial lips to pucker into that ugly duck face that was popular years ago.

Hell, if Caroline's reading books about fucking MC members, I could offer her the real deal.

My hungry gaze roams her body covered in *my* clothes. She looks so young. I'd wonder if she was legal, except while she was sleeping, I checked her ID.

Thirty-one. Only three years younger than me.

"It's unfortunate you don't read," Caroline mutters. The sweetness of her voice belies any intended insult, but Fox chokes on his drink as Tiffany's eyes narrow to slits.

Before Tiffany can unleash a retort, my Little Owl pushes her finished breakfast away and asks, "Can I go home now?"

No, you're staying with me.

That's what I want to say.

A feral part of me that only Caroline brings to life itches to lock her down as mine alone, which means where she goes, I go. But I doubt my Little Owl would agree to such terms.

Not yet, anyway.

CHAPTER EIGHT

CAROLINE

Sitting back on the barstool, the betraying heat on my cheeks lets me know I'm failing to hide my reaction to Fox and Tiffany's comments.

Yeah, I've learned to share my love of romance novels more freely with age, but hearing Tiffany's judgmental opinion stings. Because it feels like it's true, especially as a virgin at my age.

Not to mention how embarrassing it is to have Snow know what I read, too. The man's probably never lacked female companionship in his life.

"Yeah, I'll drive you home. We can take my truck instead of the bike."

I breathe a sigh of relief. Time to leave this place and never see it again.

And that's definitely not a pang of disappointment in my gut.

Hopping off the stool, I pick up my ruined clothes from where I'd placed them on the countertop, wave goodbye to Fox and Tiffany, and follow Snow out.

We pass through the communal living space I saw yesterday, except this time two women lay draped over a shirtless man on the large sectional. Clearly, they fell asleep after a wild night, judging by the lack of clothing worn by all parties.

I'm surprised my sleep wasn't disturbed outside of Snow's regular check-ups. The space is a mess of empty alcohol containers, and a muted playlist plays on the massive big-screen TV mounted to the wall.

Whatever went down last night must have been one hell of a party, and I wish I could experience the freedom of living with no inhibitions.

Unfortunately, my cousin has that covered in our family, and I've had to rescue her from more than a few messes because of it. If I decided to take a risk that led to me crashing and burning, no one would be there to pick me up because they're all burned out after helping Lauren.

I'd be on my own, so it's safer to remain in my bubble of good behavior.

Once we're alone on a front porch obviously not original to the building, Snow says, "Despite her attitude, Tiffany has a point about experience. You haven't been properly fucked if you're satisfied by only reading about it."

More humiliation burns my skin at his assertion. I almost voice my defense that virgins like me take what we can get and use toys to our advantage. But thankfully, a young man interrupts us.

I definitely don't need to share my nightly self-pleasure routine with Snow. I feel pathetic enough in front of him, thank you very much.

"Sir, Ollie needs to see you."

"Tell him to wait. I'm busy."

The man's gaze slides towards me before adding, "It's urgent. About the shop on Creighton Avenue."

Snow huffs in frustration and scratches the back of his neck before addressing me. "I'll be right back." Pointing at the guy, he warns, "Watch her, but don't fucking touch her." Then he stomps back inside.

I'm not sure the warning was necessary considering I'm not these guys' type, judging by the women I've encountered. Tiffany was tanned and toned, her chest on display behind the skimpy tank she wore, and I felt downright dowdy next to her.

Even if I wasn't wearing Snow's clothes, which miraculously dwarf my belly and hips, my daily outfit of jeans, a blouse, and a cardigan wouldn't compare.

Tiffany and the women in the living room are bikini models, while I'm the girl in the background, ensuring the photoshoot runs without issue.

Geez, I've got to get out of here.

Everywhere I turn makes me feel inferior. Like a naive kid playing at being an adult. It's unnerving since I'm used to being one of the most mature people in the room, especially when it comes to my family.

Unwilling to wait on Snow, I call Amelie. My phone's been blowing up with messages after I texted our friend group last night to let them know what happened. Technically, I'm supposed to limit screen time with my concussion, so this is my first chance to respond.

"Hey, is everything okay?" Amelie answers on the second ring.

"Yeah, I'm fine. Snow woke me up on schedule every two hours last night. My head's still a little fuzzy, but for the most part, I feel a lot better than I did yesterday."

"That's good at least. So what's it like at a real MC clubhouse?" she asks, immediately digging for the juicy details.

"It's exactly like we imagined in the books. That's why I'm calling... because I'm still here."

"Oh, your hot biker won't let you go?"

I can already imagine the vivid scenario she's envisioning of a possessive biker holding his woman captive and... Well, damn, now I'm picturing it, too, and it's fucking hot.

Too bad you're absolutely not *Snow's woman.*

"Hardly." I step away from the guy pretending like he's not listening in, embarrassed by her comment. Not to mention my wayward reaction to it. "He had some business to take care of, so I'm just waiting out here. Do you know anybody in Suitor's Crossing who could pick me up? At least I think that's where I'm at."

I turn back to my keeper and ask, "Hey, do you know the address here?"

He rattles it off, confirming my suspicions. Relaying the address to Amelie, I wait for her response.

"Yeah, my cousin Natalie lives there. Hold on while I call her to see if she's free, and then I'll get back to you, okay?"

"Sounds like a plan." We hang up, and it's not five minutes later before Amelie texts me a thumbs-up message, letting me know that her cousin will be here in fifteen minutes.

Thank God this place isn't that far out of town, despite the surroundings.

A dense forest surrounds the main warehouse and the large barn next to it. Cabins are set further back, and I assume that's where more club members live. A gravel road runs parallel to the property.

My babysitter leans against a post with his hands stuffed in his pockets. while I fiddle with my phone, urging the clock to move faster because I'm worried Snow will appear before Amelie's cousin.

Fortunately, a dust cloud billows from the gravel road, drawing nearer, and I head toward the end of the drive. Except the guy watching me starts having doubts.

"Maybe you should wait. I don't think Prez would like it if you left."

"I'm sure he won't care." He opens his mouth to counter, but I play my ace. "Besides, you really can't stop me. He told you not to touch me."

Before he can make up his mind, I take my chance and lightly jog to the spot where gravel becomes pavement and Natalie's car idles on the road. It takes two seconds for me to jump in, and she zips away before bombarding me with questions.

"What the actual fuck? How did you end up at the Reaper's Wolves clubhouse?"

Taking a deep breath and releasing it slowly, I relay what happened, and honestly, hearing it aloud, I can barely believe it myself. To think I was only trying to fill up my tires yesterday for a quick trip out of town, only to end up in an accident and spend the night in a stranger's bed.

"Holy shit!" Natalie checks her rearview mirror. "You don't think he'll come after you, do you?"

Butterflies take off in my stomach at the thought. "No way. Why bother?"

"I don't know. Amelie shared what happened that night when you all went out. It seems like there might be a connection between you two. And I've seen Snow around town. He doesn't look like the kind of guy to let something go when he wants it."

"Trust me. He doesn't want me." My voice wavers, though, as I barely recall him calling me his "baby."

But surely that's my concussion talking. Dreaming up an imaginary scenario.

As if he knows we're talking about him, a buzzing on my phone notifies me of a text. *"You left"* scrolls across the top of the screen with Snow's name. How'd he get his number into my phone?

Me: *"I was ready to go."*

I should delete his number and block him. Yet I pause when I see three dots appear on my screen as he types a response.

Honestly, I don't know what I'm waiting for. The man practically kidnapped me.

He also made sure you were okay after a terrible accident. Doesn't matter.

I can never show my face there again anyway. Besides my humiliation at breakfast, it's a freaking motorcycle clubhouse. I don't want to get mixed up in the kind of life Snow lives.

Snow: *"But I wasn't ready for you to go. I told you to wait, but it seems you like to ignore my requests. ◈"*

My mouth twitches with a smile at his emoji, though he makes a valid point. My blatant refusal to do things his way confuses me, too.

I'm a people-pleaser. I care too much about what they think of me and don't want to rock the boat. Yet here I am, rebelling against an MC president.

Maybe reading all those books with brave heroines is rubbing off on me.

Or maybe I've just lost my mind—I *have* suffered a head injury.

After sending a cute Kristen Bell shrug GIF, I turn my phone to silent.

The conversation ended... *but not blocked.*

CHAPTER NINE

CAROLINE

Snow: "LOL Have fun with your girls. Let me know when you get home safely."

"What's your man saying tonight?" Kat asks with a wink. We're gathered around the kitchen island in Beth's house, waiting for her to finish blending our margaritas for girls' night.

"He's not my man." I roll my eyes but feel a blush warm my cheeks.

Snow's been texting me ever since I left his place a week ago. I figured he'd lose interest by now, considering our differences, but he hasn't.

"If he's not *your man*," Beth says, using her fingers to create air quotes, "then why is he messaging you so much? And don't say he isn't, because your phone's gone off multiple times since you've gotten here, and anyone else you'd text is in this room."

She's got a point; my circle of friends is small. We're only missing Amelie because she had to work at the last minute, and she's notoriously bad at responding to texts.

"People can talk without being an item... I'm not even sure I'd call us friends. I don't know what we are."

Which is the truth.

He lives an hour away in Suitor's Crossing, so it's not easy to just meet for coffee or whatever. Plus, I'm not exactly sure what kind of motorcycle club he's in—if they're a one-percenter or a legitimate club that stays on the right side of the law.

At first, I planned on ignoring his messages, figuring they wouldn't last long without me continuing the conversation. But Snow pressed on and kept asking questions about myself.

It felt rude not to respond, which is ridiculous, I know. But I'd tell him what he'd want to know, and that's what our conversations have been like.

Every once in a while, he drops in a personal tidbit about himself, but otherwise, he's been completely focused on me. Which is flattering, I admit, but maybe a little stalkerish now that I think about it—if one can be a stalker when your stalkee willingly gives you the information.

"I definitely think he wants to be 'more than friends' as much as he messages you, and at least he's being clear about his interest. That's more than I can say for about eighty percent of the single male population," Kat chimes in, and we all nod in agreement.

While I haven't dated much, I've heard enough of Kat's horror stories about men—not to mention my own confusion when it comes to a guy's interest.

Beth pours each of us a strawberry margarita, and we bring all of our snacks to the living room, where we get comfortable.

"So..." Kat starts. I know something crazy is about to come out of her mouth when I see that mischievous look in her eyes. "I know you're not friends or whatever, but if you were, what would you let him do to you?"

I choke on my drink, causing both of them to laugh at my reaction. "What?" I gasp out.

"Oh, come on! We know you're the kinkiest of us all, even if you happen to be the least experienced. Don't forget who introduced us to our book boyfriends and brought the spice into our lives. And he's a sexy badass! I know you've had some dirty thoughts, so spill!"

Now, I know I'm hard-core blushing. In fact, my whole body feels on fire because I've definitely dreamt about Snow, but I can't share those. They'd read too much into it when I definitely *cannot* get involved with him.

It's not my fault that my brain can't be controlled at night.

"I haven't thought about anything except to wonder when he'll stop bothering me." I lie straight through my teeth.

"Really?" Beth raises an eyebrow in disbelief.

"Really."

"You haven't had *any* late-night fantasies? Haven't dreamed of him riding up on his Harley, shirtless, and taking you to bed?" Kat pushes, shoving a handful of M&Ms into her mouth.

"Nope." Although now I wonder if she has, and a curl of possessiveness unwinds in my stomach before I squash it.

Snow's not mine, and I don't want him to be.

Correction: he can't *be.*

Even if he wasn't part of an MC, I doubt I'd feel differently. He's still a hot Army veteran who intimidates me with his sheer size and presence.

I didn't think Snow could get any sexier. Then he revealed his past military service, and now, visions of him in uniform *and* his leather MC cut fill my fantasies.

Totally inappropriate and never going to happen fantasies because we come from different worlds.

For whatever reason, Snow seems to have forgotten that fact and his warning from the first night we met.

I'd like to believe it's because he's so enchanted by me, but let's get real. This is probably a passing fancy for him.

Maybe a sense of responsibility lingers due to the accident and my concussion. Maybe he's just assuring himself that I'm fine because he's a natural protector. Either way, his interest will fade eventually.

Especially when a more suitable woman comes along—something the clubhouse seemed full of during my stay.

Beth sets down her drink with a sigh. "Alright. Fine. You don't have feelings for Snow. Guess we'll have to take your word for it, and if that's the case, then I have good news." She pulls out her phone and starts scrolling.

"What kind of news?" I take another sip of my drink, thankful that this line of questioning seems to be over.

I don't like my friends nosing into my business when it comes to Snow. It's hard enough dealing with feelings that crop up on my own. I don't need them needling me, causing them to resurface.

"There's this guy in my volunteer group, and we got to talking about dating and how difficult it is to find normal people. Because it can be wild out there. Anyway, I thought this might be a good opportunity to set you up on an actual date."

She looks at me expectantly, and I'm not sure what to think. Kat and Beth are always saying they want to set me up with guys, but they've never actually followed through.

"My first question is, why aren't you trying to date him?"

Beth's pretty, and they already have volunteering in common.

"Oh, we're just friends." She waves off my question. "I asked him if he was interested in being set up, and he was hesitant at first, but then I showed him your picture. He said, and I quote, 'Damn, she's hot!' Then agreed to the date!"

"What pic did you show him?" I'm curious to know what he found hot because I don't have that many pictures that qualify. Although, in general, whenever I'm having a good day, I'd say I'm cute, never the hot type.

"The one after Sara Bareilles's concert." Beth shows a picture of the four of us standing in front of the stage with big smiles. I admit I looked good with skinny jeans and a v-neck tee knotted in front.

"Yeah, but there are four of us there. Are you sure he was talking about me?"

"Of course! I said 'the brunette' and pointed at you."

"Oh."

I don't really know what to say. I've gone thirty-one years with basically no male interest in me, and now it seems I have two possible suitors. I'm not sure I'm ready for it.

"Oh?" Kat mimics me. "What's the matter? It's about damn time you got out there! If the hot biker dude isn't doing it for you, then maybe this guy will be a match. Did he ask for her number?" Kat turns to Beth, and they start gushing about possible dates and what I should wear.

I lean back against the couch and pull my legs further under me, like making myself into a ball will somehow take away my nerves at this turn of events.

"I told him I had to check with Caro first. So, can I give him your number? Tell him it's okay to set up a date?" Both of their eyes are wide with excited anticipation.

They're right. I need to put myself out there.

Part of the reason I haven't had a lot of experience is because of how shy and awkward I can be. I never know what to say and tend to run in the other direction when an attractive man approaches.

You didn't run when Snow appeared, my brain sing-songs.

I didn't really have a choice in those situations, I reason.

Yes, you did, and you stood toe-to-toe with him. Plus, you're still talking to him.

I'm writing to him; there's a difference.

"Earth to Caro? What's it gonna be?"

I'm shaken out of my argument with myself and cautiously give the green light. Hopefully, I won't regret this decision.

THE OFFICE KITCHEN is empty the next morning as I wait for the Keurig to heat, reeling from my decision to be set up by Beth.

After she gave Tyler my number, he texted me, asking if I wanted to go out this Friday. Which means two men have messaged me within the past twelve hours—two more than I've ever had in my life.

I sent a "thumbs up" emoji to accept the date, but I'm still hesitant about the whole ordeal. He's texted a couple of times, but not nearly as much as Snow has. And while I shouldn't be comparing the two of them, the difference is glaring.

As if reading my mind, my phone vibrates. Pulling it out, a message from Snow flashes on the screen.

Snow: *"I'll be back in town tomorrow. When can I see you?"*

My eyes widen at the question. Although we've been texting a lot, I'm not sure it's a good idea to hang out. What would we even talk about? Our conversations so far are reaching the end of the "getting to know you" stuff, which leaves us with things we have in common.

Also known as: *not much*.

He's a Harley-riding, active outdoorsman—a freaking mountain man based on his interests. I prefer staying inside, cozied up with a book. He's traveled the world during his military service, while I've never ventured outside of the country's borders.

He's experienced, and I'm not. In more ways than one.

If we meet in person again, Snow's bound to figure out how unexciting I truly am, and the thought of watching his interest turn to boredom before my very eyes sends a shaft of fear and humiliation through my gut.

Living in this cyber world of texting, where he's kept at a distance, is safer. Allows me to pretend I'm brave and attractive to a man like him without actually risking much of my heart.

The Keurig groans as coffee spits out of the dispenser, and the smell of coffee comforts me as I shove my phone back in my pocket without responding. Steam rises from my mug as hot liquid meets the ice cubes I put in earlier, preferring iced coffee that's drowned in French vanilla creamer.

On the way back to my desk, I see my coworker Lindy just getting in. Since I was the last one hired at the company, I'm in the first cubicle at the front of the building, which is annoying.

I'm expected to answer every doorbell-ringing visitor like a glorified desk clerk rather than them hiring someone specifically to greet clients.

"Hey!" I wave a hand in greeting as I observe her ruffled state—wind-blown hair, hands juggling a coffee and breakfast bag along with her purse. "Was traffic crazy?"

Lindy pauses, seemingly startled by my question. "Um, yeah, it was terrible." She scurries past me when I notice a purple mark peeking out of the neckline of her shirt.

"I think you've got something here." I gesture to my neck, and she glances down, brushing the shirt aside. That's when I notice that the mark extends out into yellows and greens.

"Lindy, what happened?" I ask in shock, setting my coffee mug down. The bruise is large and ugly-looking, even if it seems to be healing.

"Oh, nothing. I must've bumped into something. I haven't even noticed it," she says quickly. Her eyes avoid mine as she fidgets on one foot, then the other.

"Really? It's pretty large. Are you sure you're okay?"

Lindy and I aren't super close, but we always chat when we bump into each other, and she's one of the few people at work close to my age. We actually started around the same time but in separate departments.

"I'm fine, really. I just need to get to my desk. See you later." She rushes away, and what looks to be an older mark on the side of her neck catches my attention.

Frowning, I take a seat at my desk and wiggle the mouse to wake up the computer monitor.

I'm not sure if I've been oblivious to any bruises before or if today she didn't do a great job of hiding them. Either way, concern fills me at the possibility of how she's getting the injuries.

Stop it. Maybe she's just clumsy.

My mind likes to leap to worst-case scenarios—the bane of being an enneagram six. It's probably nothing, and she just bruises easily from the lightest of touches.

Typing in my password, I start working on my to-do list and try to push aside my worry for Lindy. If she needs help, there are probably people she's closer to that she could ask for aid from. She doesn't need an overly-concerned co-worker barging into her affairs.

Doesn't stop the sense of responsibility I feel to act, though.

CHAPTER TEN

CAROLINE

The timer goes off for the chocolate chip cookies baking in honor of Hallmark starting their fall harvest movies. I'm not usually a baker, but I figured it'd be fun to make tonight a special occasion. It's Friday night, I've got my pumpkin candle lit, cozy pajamas on, and I'm about to enjoy a sweet romance.

A wild night, for sure.

This is why I'm single and wouldn't fit into Snow's MC life. A Hallmark movie premiere is more exciting than partying. And life at the clubhouse seemed like one big party from the little I'd seen and the pounding music I'd heard the few times Snow woke me up that night.

Carefully removing the cookies from the oven, I take them to the living room, where I set them down on a pot holder laid out to avoid burning the table. The beginning credits for the movie start as orange and red leaves fill the screen, and I rush to grab a drink before cuddling under a blanket on the couch.

I'm halfway through the movie when a knock at the door startles me, sending my heart into a panic as a thousand scary scenarios flash through my paranoid mind.

It's nine at night. Who could be outside? Should I pretend I'm not home? It's not like my TV's super loud, and the only light's coming from my candle.

The banging on my door sounds again, more insistent this time.

Maybe something's wrong? Holding my breath, I creep to the door and peek through the peephole, inhaling sharply when a familiar form blocks the view to the parking lot.

It's Snow.

I never responded to his message from yesterday, and I don't know what to do now.

"Open up, Little Owl. I know you're in there."

His words send a jolt through me, and I'm embarrassed by my own actions. I'm a grown-ass woman. I can answer the damn door without hyperventilating. Gathering myself, I unlock the door and inch it open.

"What are you doing here?"

He steps forward, forcing the door wider to allow him entry. "Since you never responded yesterday, I thought I'd stop by tonight. Did you think if you ignored me long enough, I'd just forget about you? Impossible, baby."

Scarlet shame blooms on my skin because he isn't far off in his estimation.

Snow's dark jeans and leather boots are covered in dust, while his black hair is mussed like it is after he removes his helmet. His beard looks wilder, as if he hasn't had time to maintain it, making him look even more like the dangerous MC president.

God, he looks good even as an unkempt mess.

"I didn't know what to say." Honesty's the best policy, right? "I don't think it's a good idea for us to hang out."

"And why's that?" he asks, his voice low as he presses closer until I've backed into the door behind me.

The smell of gasoline and nature wafts from him, teasing my nose with the contradicting scents—Snow's a biker mountain man with all the burly protective traits you could want, and it's so unfair that I'm too afraid to risk anything with him.

Straightening, I try to stand strong as my hands clench and unclench at my sides.

"I think it's pretty obvious..."

He's part of a mysterious, most likely illegal underworld, while I live in the relative safety of the law-abiding world.

"Is it?" He leans in until our mouths are an inch apart, and I struggle to focus.

I've never been this close to a man, and it's making me nervous and excited. Flustering my thoughts like nothing ever has before—except maybe every other time I've been near Snow.

"The only thing obvious to me is that I've spent the last twenty-four hours thinking of seeing you tonight. Imagining what I'd do when I saw you. You know what I imagined, baby?"

My breathing stutters at the desire flaring in his silver eyes.

What is happening?

This can't be real life, especially not for a boring goody two shoes like me. I've never even gone on a date! And now I have this sexy but intimidating man in my apartment declaring his intentions.

You mean his desires. What happens after he gets what he wants?

"Snow..." Before I can figure out what to say, his mouth covers mine in a rough kiss—his beard scratching my cheek—as I gasp in shock.

His tongue stakes a claim I'm not prepared for.

All my life I've dreamed of what my first kiss would be like—tentative and shy, slow and sweet—suited to the type of man I thought I'd be with. But this is nothing like those fantasies.

It's hard and bruising, fierce with passion, and I don't know how to handle it.

This is better than all of my dreams put together and will, no doubt, provide ample fodder for even more imaginary illicit scenarios between the two of us. My fingers dig into his broad shoulders as my core clenches in anticipation—dampening with arousal to ease Snow's access.

You are absolutely not sleeping with Snow tonight!

Or ever...

But my resolve weakens with each confident swipe of his tongue on mine, every playful nip at my lips. The heavy weight of his body holds me firmly against the door, pressing deep so no part of me is separate from him. Calloused palms slide underneath my top, causing me to jerk at the new sensation.

Unfamiliar feelings rush through my body, and I feel like I'm going to burst into flame at any second. I want to give in so badly. I'm desperate to let him have his wicked way with me.

However wrong it may be.

Snow's mouth moves lower, licking before sucking hard on the side of my neck, which shoots a firebolt straight between my thighs. A slight rock of my hips has me riding his thick arousal, and an involuntary moan escapes me.

Get control. You need to stop this.

Before I go too far and get too deep.

Trying to catch my breath, I choke out his name. "Snow..."

"When we're like this, baby, it's Logan."

Logan.

I realize I didn't even know his first name until now, yet I'm letting him pin me to the door. Letting his hands wander over my bare skin. It's like a bucket of ice water was tossed in my face as I freeze.

"Logan, stop." As difficult as it is, I push against him. "This absolutely cannot happen."

Reluctantly, he puts some space between us, though I'm still caged within his arms. "Why not? What's wrong?" His gunmetal gray eyes study me, confusion and lust warring within them.

"I told you we shouldn't hang out. You even warned me away at the bar. Which means we can't... we shouldn't... um..." I gesture between us, trying to convey my meaning. Coherent thoughts refuse to materialize as my mind attempts to clear the fog it's mired in.

"Make out? Fuck?"

A rush of heat surges forward at the crude term.

We *definitely* can't *fuck.*

"Right," I agree, anxiously running my hands through my hair unsuccessfully. *Damn knotty curls.* "I appreciate how you helped after the crash, but I'm fine now, so there's really no reason for us to keep in touch."

"We've been 'in touch' for over a week now. What's changed? Too afraid to talk to me in person?"

God, yes.

Instead, I say, "I'm sorry if I led you on. It felt rude not to reply to any of your messages."

He stiffens, and I brace for his response, wincing at the tense clenching of his jaw. "You're saying you only responded out of politeness?"

Well, not entirely true, but maybe it's best if I let him believe that.

"Yes," I confirm, holding my breath.

Logan stares at me for long seconds, analyzing my expression with narrowed eyes. I try to appear stern and steadfast, and just as I think he's going to call me on the lie, he rears back like he suddenly can't bear to touch me—the fire of desire manifesting to scorch him with my rejection.

"Fine. That's how you want it to be? I won't bother you anymore." He moves me to the side and storms out.

Almost as quickly as he appeared, he's gone, and a motorcycle roars to life outside.

I lock the door and stare blankly at the movie playing on the TV. It's the end, and the camera's panning away as the couple kiss in a pumpkin patch. But I don't care about them anymore.

My problems won't magically fix themselves into a fairytale ending.

Slumping onto the couch, Snow's easy acceptance niggles at the back of my mind. *That was easier than I thought it would be.* For some reason, I thought Snow... *Logan* would push harder—argue more. Instead, he accepted my excuse and left.

Disappointment sits like lead in my stomach. My hopeless romantic and totally unwise heart wanted him to fight for me, which is ridiculous. He's no good for me.

I pushed him away for a reason. Because we'd never work long-term. Because I could never fit into his MC world.

He's just a novelty that I need to get over ASAP.

Maybe my blind date with Tyler will help.

Doubtful, I sigh in frustration before sitting up straight and rewinding to where I left off in the movie, determined to enjoy the rest of my night and forget about Logan Snow.

This short, odd chapter in our story is over.

Time to get back to my regular, normal life.

Don't forget boring, too!

CHAPTER ELEVEN

SNOW

Cool mountain hair whips across my face as I ride back to the clubhouse after Caroline kicked me out of her apartment.

That's not what I expected when I'd decided to visit her instead of going straight home earlier. All I'd thought about today was her. Hell, my Little Owl hasn't left my mind since the day I tried warning her away from me at No Man's Land.

But, apparently, the feeling isn't mutual, since she pushed me away with some nonsense about being polite. Her messages were more than good manners. You don't spend hours talking with someone out of duty.

No matter how much she denies it, Caroline's as drawn to me as I am to her. Her response to our kiss proved that. It just pisses me off that she won't admit it.

Which is why I stormed out after saying I wouldn't bother her anymore—not really meaning those words, but angry and hurt at her rejection.

It'd been a long day inspecting another robbery at one of our businesses. After a threatening call to Breaker, he swore the Ghost Rider MC had nothing to do with it, though I don't put much trust in his word. Because if he's not harassing us, then that means we're being targeted on two fronts when I've already got enough problems to deal with.

Like my Little Owl.

I park my bike in front of the small cabin at the back of the property, separate from everyone else. While I mainly live at the clubhouse—available at a moment's notice—I keep this refuge to myself for the times I need total isolation.

It's bare-bones inside: a bed, a beat-up couch, and a wobbly dining table with two chairs. Nothing fancy. But it does the trick when I need an escape from the noise and partying happening at the main house.

Walking inside, I toss my wallet on the table and strip down for a hot shower, imagining the scent of cookies clinging to me as if Caroline were here.

Damn, she'd smelled sweet.

Tasted even sweeter.

Adjusting the shower dials, I step into the tub and let the water wash away the sweat and dirt of today's ride.

My hair and beard get a good scrubbing as I tug on the unruly length, knowing I need a trim, before moving on to grab the body wash. When I'm done and the water's starting to cool, I finally take my cock in hand and begin stroking.

My head rests on a forearm placed on the wet tile as my eyes close and I envision Caroline as she was tonight.

Her plaid sleep shorts and matching top with the first few buttons undone across her generous tits, mahogany curls tossed up in an unraveling bun. And the reason for her nickname: those glasses that magnify her blue eyes.

With a groan, my pace increases, imagining her small hands replacing my larger ones. I'd guide her—show her how to grip firmly and harshly squeeze my steel cock with every stroke—since I know she's innocent. That was one of the first questions I'd asked when we started texting.

I remember the burgeoning jealousy as I asked if there were any men I needed to know about, then the wave of relief when she'd confessed there'd never been anyone—I'd be her first.

"Caroline..." Her name echoes across the bathroom walls as I picture her gaze on mine, mouth swollen from our kisses, but then a cool breeze skims over me before another hand joins mine.

My eyes shoot open, and a naked Tiffany fills my vision.

"What the fuck?" I shout, slapping her hand away. Caroline really has me wrapped around her little finger if I didn't notice someone creeping into my home after years standing guard in the military.

Steam escapes the stall as Tiffany pulls the shower curtain further back. "I saw you drive past the clubhouse and knew you were coming here. You didn't come back with the rest of the guys earlier. I've been waiting for you."

She reaches for my cock again, which is quickly deflating with her intrusion. "Let me show you how much I've missed you."

Too bad she's not the woman I want touching me.

"You thought it'd be okay to break into my fucking home like it's your own? You must be out of your damn mind!" I shout, snagging the one towel I keep here and escaping the bathroom.

Wrapping it around my hips, I run a hand through my wet hair. What else can go wrong tonight?

Even my fucking daydream of Caroline gets ruined.

"I wanted to see you." Tiffany follows me into the living room, tracking puddles of water behind her.

Crossing her arms over her fake tits, she continues, "Fox said you went to see that girl, the one who thinks reading about sex is better than actually fucking. And judging by the state I found you, I guess she still feels that way."

"Don't talk about Caroline, and don't come here again unless you want to be banned from the property. You're *not* my fucking woman, and we've got plenty of women to take your place. Trust me, you won't be missed." I point to the door—my message clear.

Tiffany ignores me and drops her arms so a hand draws a line down between her breasts and over a pierced belly button until she reaches her shaved pussy.

Pouting, she plays with herself and says, "You don't mean that. We used to have fun, Snow. Don't you remember? I can fuck you better than little Virgin Mary ever could."

Like a bull seeing red, fury erupts at the insult to Caroline, and my jaw tightens as I grit out, "That was your last warning."

Grabbing her arm and dragging her to the door, I pick up the clothes she left strewn around the room as I go. I don't have time for this shit.

Tiffany stumbles behind me. "You're not gonna let me get dressed first? You can't throw me out like this!"

"Watch me." I toss the clothes, then her, outside as I shove the door open.

Like I give a damn that it's forty degrees outside and she's naked. Maybe the chill will knock some sense into her.

She rushes to gather her things as she spouts off curses, but I turn around and lock the door, ignoring the tantrum.

Heading to the fridge, I pop open a beer and down it in one gulp.

How could one night go downhill so fast?

All I wanted was an evening spent with my Little Owl. Instead, I get ambushed in the shower by a woman who refuses to take a hint.

Exhaustion weighs on me as the events of the day catch up to my body, and I decide it's best to sleep it off because tomorrow's got to be better.

Maybe I'll even get lucky and dream of Caroline... or figure out my next move.

Because even though I'm frustrated with my woman, I still want her. That fact hit home when Tiffany showed up. I'm tired of women like Tiff, the ones only interested in how much power fucking a club president gets them.

Caroline doesn't care about that.

In our text conversations, we talked about all sorts of things: favorite sports teams, what it was like growing up, the books she was reading. Topics that never came up with Tiffany or any other woman.

Like a breath of fresh air, she'd revived me, offered a reprieve from the issues our club's facing at the moment. And as I drift to sleep, I vow that I won't give her up without a fight.

On paper, we may not make sense—the veteran biker and the innocent civilian—but I'm determined to have Caroline as my own.

Suitor's Crossing is known for *heart sparks*? Well, hell, then I think she's mine.

Because I've never felt this type of obsession for a woman before, and it's only growing stronger each time I'm near her.

CHAPTER TWELVE

CAROLINE

I double-check my outfit in the mirror as I wait for Tyler to get here. Tonight's our date, and I'm nervous.

Unfortunately, our texts haven't made me more comfortable with the idea of going out with him, since they've remained pretty surface-level. But I'm hoping our in-person conversations flow easier.

It also doesn't help that my mind's been obsessed with Logan. The absence of his messages. His fiery kiss. The brief look of pain that crossed his face after I rejected him.

I can't shake a sense of guilt for how I treated him.

Why am I such a coward?

"Stop it," I tell myself in the mirror. Now's not the time for self-denigration. I need to get excited, feel confident for this date.

Smoothing sweaty hands down my skinny jeans, I turn to the side, trying to imagine what Tyler will see. The navy tank I chose is tucked into the waist while the vee at the neck reveals some cleavage.

I'm trying to step out of my comfort zone and put myself out there, but I wonder if he's going to see sexy curves or not.

As a solid size eighteen and the opposite type of woman I usually see "get the guy," I worry he'll be disappointed. A lifetime of watching models win the man in every romcom and TV show has me doubting my allure, despite knowing those are all fictional characters.

Though it's not like anyone's ever rejected me in real life due to my weight. Bolstered by the realization, I grab my cardigan for a little bit of protection and head to the living room.

Thoughts of Logan wander into my mind again as I sit on the couch listening for a car to pull up. Our kiss has featured in a lot of my dreams, day and night, and I can't shake the regret I have from turning him away. He made me feel sexy and wanted, but does that overcome all of our differences?

Plus, the small detail on whether his club is legit or not remains a mystery.

Staring at my phone, I turn it over in my hands, trying to figure out what to do. To be fair, I don't know for sure that Logan's into anything illegal. I just assumed based on my limited knowledge of motorcycle clubs. But would a military veteran really leave the service just to break the law?

Would knowing they're totally above board really change anything? A dangerous aura still surrounds him.

Groaning at how complicated my life's become, I resolve to not think about Logan, our kiss, or anything pertaining to MCs tonight.

Focus on your date.

This could be the start of something great if I let myself believe it.

With that positive outlook buoying my nerves, my phone buzzes with a text.

Tyler: *"Hey, I'm outside."*

A frisson of disappointment runs through me, though I try not to let the fact that he didn't come to the door affect me. I'm just being old-fashioned. No need to judge the guy before I even meet him.

Grabbing my purse and keys, I steel myself for whatever the night holds.

Thirty minutes later, we're in the next town over and park next to an industrial building. A crowd of people head to the entrance in tee shirts with two men on the front.

I release a relieved breath, grateful we're finally here after the awkward and mostly silent drive. Something seemed off with Tyler as I tried to make small talk, but I'm not sure what it could be.

Obviously, I don't know him well, but at least in his messages, he gave more than one-word answers.

Tucking a piece of hair behind my ear, I focus on the front of the building to stop my insecurities from overwhelming me. It's hard not to assume Tyler's attitude has something to do with me, but it's not like this is a total blind date. Beth showed him my picture. I couldn't have been a surprise.

Think positively.

Just because things aren't going well doesn't mean they can't turn around.

After getting out of the car, I struggle to keep up with Tyler as he pushes through throngs of people, until we're in a fast-moving line to a booth set up on the side of the building.

We're at an MMA fight if the posters hanging on either side of the windows are anything to go by. An odd choice for a first date. But maybe he's a huge fan and wants to make sure I know that?

"One ticket," Tyler says to the attendant.

Guess I'm buying my own ticket.

More disappointment settles in my stomach. Sighing, I step forward to pay before following him inside. People surround a giant cage that sits center stage, and we push towards the front where Tyler finally stops.

Standing beside him, I ask, "Who are you rooting for?" I know absolutely nothing about MMA, but it feels weird being on a date and not talking.

He huffs in annoyance. "Look, somehow Beth's wires got crossed. You're not the girl from the picture." He gestures at my body before continuing, "You're not my type. I don't date fat chicks. You can leave if you want."

His callous attitude stabs me in the gut. Surely, this can't be real. "Why did you bother bringing me here if you didn't want to?"

"What was I supposed to do? Lock the doors before you got in? Besides, I thought I'd do you a favor and stick it out, but your talking is annoying, too. I'm sure there's an Uber outside to take you home."

He shrugs like it's not his problem, clearly wanting me to go away, before turning back to face the cage.

My chest tightens as the air dams up in my lungs, making it difficult to breathe. The crowd blurs as tears well up. Blinking rapidly, I try to regulate my body from the rush of emotions assaulting me.

Fat and annoying.

His words echo in my brain.

How he was able to pinpoint the exact insult to decimate my self-esteem is mind-boggling. The comment about my weight stings, but it's his disgust with my "annoying" talking that has the past threatening to swallow me whole.

Because Lauren used to call me that.

My cousin always had something to say while I politely listened, rarely feeling the need to interject with my own opinion. However, on the odd occasion when I had something exciting of my own to share, she'd shut me down.

"Shut up, Caro. You're being annoying."

Which is why I prefer staying in the background where I can't be a nuisance. Why I don't want to stick out and call attention to myself.

Tapping out a shaky message to the friend group chat, I pray someone's able to pick me up soon. I don't want to grab an Uber where my composure might break, and I cry in front of a stranger.

Because my worst fears are literally happening, and I'm trapped here, surrounded by strangers until someone rescues me.

CHAPTER THIRTEEN

Snow

I lean against the wall at the edge of the crowd, idly waiting for the event to begin. A spat of lighter weight fighters will compete before the main attraction—Slater Hughes versus Danny Gonzalez—starts.

Some of the guys thought it'd be fun to blow off steam by attending because there's been another break-in at our strip club in Everton. And I'm about to shove this truce up Breaker's ass if I find out it's his club doing it again.

"Anything on the surveillance footage?" I ask Ollie, who's lounging beside me, more concerned with the video on his phone than the fight.

"No. Sorry, boss. Somehow they're bypassing our security." Ollie looks like he wants to say something else.

"Spit it out."

"Well, I hate to think about it, but... I'm starting to wonder if this isn't an inside job."

"One of our guys?"

"How else would the thieves be able to bypass our security every time? Only someone who knows the layout and codes could do that. It might have been Breaker's team doing it at first, but I think they had help."

"So we've got a rat in our midst."

Hard to believe.

The guys are all former military, and we look after each other. To learn that one of them isn't loyal and actively sabotaging us is a hard pill to swallow. Would any of them really turn against us?

"See what you can find out. Bring Fox in on this if you need help."

"Sure thing, boss."

"I want to find out who's orchestrating these break-ins to steal our shit and put this to bed."

Frustration licks along my veins, which is why I agreed to join the guys tonight.

Despite my reluctance, it's good to get out of the clubhouse. A few days have passed, and this break-in heightens the bad mood I'm still in because of Caroline. I can't figure out how to overcome her dismissal, not when I don't understand the reason behind it.

Because her kisses and body language don't lie. She wants me just as badly as I want her.

Studying the throng of MMA fans, a familiar face catches my eye. Straightening, my gaze narrows, following my Little Owl as she trails behind some preppy jock.

What the hell?

Caroline doesn't belong here. Especially not with another man.

When they get as close as possible to the cage, a conversation ensues before Caroline whips around and pushes her way back the way they came.

This is a smaller fight in High Ridge—a more intimate venue—which makes it standing room only and harder to follow someone, but I track her like a hawk until she finally nears a thinning of the crowd. Moving towards her, my anger grows the closer I get.

Why the hell is she here with that douche? She was kissing *me* a week ago!

But as I near my Little Owl, I see tears glistening on her cheeks, and my frustration immediately turns to a killing fury over whatever that prick's done to her.

"Caroline?" I reach out, but at the sound of her name, she jerks away before my hand touches her arm.

"What... What are you doing here?" she stumbles over her words, quickly wiping at her eyes as if I can't see her crying right in front of me.

Circling her wrist, I pull her behind me until we're in a secluded corner separated from prying eyes by a stacked wall of punching bags.

This building doubles as a gym, so they must have emptied all the equipment out before erecting the stage. Providing the perfect hidden alcove for me to question my Little Owl.

"I should be asking you the same thing. You don't belong here."

"Trust me, I know," she says as she stares down at her feet, curls falling forward to hide her face. My finger tilts her chin up, so we're looking at each other eye to eye, disliking the barrier.

"So, what are you doing here, and why are you crying?"

"It's nothing. Don't worry about it." Her hands play with the buttons on her cardigan in a nervous gesture.

"Baby, I'm not letting you leave without knowing what's going on. So, you might as well tell me before I have Fox drag that bastard you came with back here, and I find out my own way. What's it gonna be?"

Caroline's eyes widen at the threat, exaggerating her owl-like appearance behind those glasses, and her chest rises as she inhales a deep breath before slowly releasing it.

"Beth set me up on a date... And it's not working out." She rushes through the words like that'll keep me from hearing them.

Flames kindle in my blood at the thought of her dating another man. I know I have no right to her, but I can't shake the possessiveness I feel when it comes to my Little Owl.

"Why isn't it working out?'

"He... he's just not interested." Another tear slips out at the choked answer.

Like pulling teeth, I ask another question. We can stand here all night if we have to. I'm going to get to the bottom of what he did to hurt my woman.

"What do you mean he's not interested?"

What kind of idiot wouldn't want her? She's perfect—smart, beautiful, sweet. The kind of girl every man desires. Me, especially.

"I'm not his type, okay? I don't want to talk about it anymore." Her mouth forms a straight line of refusal as her eyes dart to the side. She looks like a bunny about to bolt the clutches of a hungry wolf, but this wolf's determined to never release her from his protection.

"Well, I do. He made you cry, and that's not something I'm gonna ignore."

Caroline finally meets my eyes, and a spark of anger glimmers in her blue irises. At least I'm getting her to feel something other than sadness. I can't stand seeing her tears.

"Too damn bad. This night's already been a nightmare, and I want it to end. I'm not his type. End of story."

"That's what I don't get. You're not his type? You're a goddamn dream."

Her brows wrinkle in confusion as a mocking laugh cuts through the air. "I'm no one's dream."

"Wrong, baby."

The lights go down as loud music shakes the walls and cheers go up as the fighters are announced. Perfect timing because now it's like we're in our own little cocoon, closed off from prying eyes. Though I know Fox and Timber are aware of our location, they won't bother us.

Cupping both her cheeks, I brush my mouth over a salty tear. "I dream of you every night, think of you every day. You're never far from my mind. Why do you think I messaged you so much? Like a damn schoolboy with his first crush."

My lips drift over her tear tracks, desperate to absorb the pain. Her lashes flutter shut and a shudder travels down her body at the gentle touch. "I told you that you're mine, and I don't lie."

"But why? It doesn't make sense. We're too different, and I'm nothing special." Disbelief rings loud and clear as her hand rests over my heart.

Worried she's about to push me away, I press closer to anchor her against the wall.

Softness cushions me, and I wish I could sink into her and stay forever. Wish I could make her see what I see.

"You're light and sunshine wrapped in the sexiest fucking curves. Curves that belong underneath me as I show you just how perfect you are," I growl. "That asshole doesn't deserve you."

"Logan..."

I quiet her with my mouth, not ready to hear a word of protest. My tongue meets her shy one, and the innocent action still surprises me. If I'd met her before now, you can be damn sure I would've kissed her as often as I could and had her in my bed in no time flat.

Of course, I haven't had much luck so far, but hopefully, I can convince her to take a chance on me soon.

Drawing back, I graze a hand down her neck and notice the fading love bite I left from the other night. Another possessive streak shoots through me, stronger than ever.

Placing my mouth over the spot, I suck hard again, never wanting her without some piece of me marking her—serving as a warning sign to anyone who dares to come near her that she's got a man. The animalistic reaction should concern me, but I can't shake the compulsion.

A whimper escapes as her hands tangle in my hair, but she's not shoving me away.

A small victory.

The spectacle in the center of the room holds everyone's attention as another roar rises from the crowd. Dim light flashes over the deep red bruise forming on Caroline's delicate skin.

Satisfaction fills me.

Mine.

"Let me prove I'm right, baby. Give yourself to me. Right here. Right now."

It's a bold request—allowing me to pleasure her while hordes of potential witnesses stand not ten feet away—but I'm practically salivating at the chance to taste that sweet pussy scalding my dick through our clothing.

I plant my palms against the wall on either side of her head and flex my hips, driving my hard arousal into the cleft of her thighs. Caroline gasps, shifting to her tiptoes to give me better access as her head rests on the cold concrete.

Desperate need has replaced the sadness from earlier, and I rock into her again, pressing my advantage.

"Bet I can make you come just like this, Little Owl. Just my cock rubbing against your pussy as you soak our jeans with your arousal." My teeth nip at her bottom lip, laving the bite with my tongue a second later. "But I'm a greedy man. Because you know what I want?"

Caroline shakes her head. "N... no..."

"I want you to ride my tongue in front of all these people. I need to feel the clench of your cunt as I swallow every last drop of your cream. Lapping your pretty little clit and..."

"Okay!" A mewl of distress falls from her lips. "Yes, please..."

Toying with the vee of her collar, I ask, "Are you sure? There's no going back after this, Caroline. You'll be mine—permanently."

And I can't wait.

My best friend Austin will probably give me shit about falling for *heart sparks* after voicing my doubts that soulmates exist, but I couldn't care less. Now, we'll be able to double date instead of me being the third wheel with him and Luna.

"I'm tired of fighting this, Logan." Caroline glances up at me and bites her lip before whispering, "Just don't make me regret it, okay?"

"Never."

Everything happens at once.

My mouth claims hers again as my fingers stretch the neckline of her shirt aside to expose one silk-covered breast. Circling the peaked nipple over the fabric, I swallow Caroline's moan before slipping beneath her bra to pinch the taut bud.

My large palms barely span her generous tits, and I curse our need for discretion. If we weren't in the middle of a packed gym, I'd rip her shirt overhead so I can freely witness the plumping of her nipples beneath my fingers, the soft peach of her skin deepening to warm pinks and reds.

Soon, I promise myself.

Soon, my Little Owl will be writhing naked on my bed, vulnerable to my ravenous gaze.

"...and here comes your reigning champion, Slater Hughes!"

The echoing announcement reminds me that we're working with borrowed time as the final fight of the night begins.

Fiddling with the button on her jeans, I abandon her breasts to drag her jeans low enough to expose her panty-clad pussy. They cling to her round ass, causing me to wiggle them with more force before the fabric finally releases its prize and obeys.

"Damn, baby, one of these days I'm gonna have to bend you over just to admire that juicy ass of yours while I fuck this hot cunt. You're just soft and curvy all over, aren't you?"

Soft and curvy and all mine.

CHAPTER FOURTEEN

CAROLINE

The admiration in Logan's tone eclipses Tyler's earlier aversion to my body. Here's a man who desires me as I am, and it's a heady experience. Especially when I'm half-exposed to an entire crowd of MMA fans.

I can't believe I'm doing this—a "conscientious" goody two shoes like me who prefers to fade into the background. If anyone caught sight of us now, fading into obscurity would be impossible. I'd be front and center, the woman who let the sexy MC president fuck her in public.

Geez, even thinking it gets me all hot and bothered rather than freaked out.

Logan's warm breath seeps through my panties as his mouth covers the damp fabric. His tongue presses the cotton deeper between my pussy lips before his mouth finds my clit, sucking it through the thin barrier.

"Oh, god..." The sensation's dulled, though not by much. It's a teasing pressure, and I wonder if Logan plans on making me come just like this.

My bunched jeans trap me in an awkward position where I can't spread my legs much further to give him better access—no matter how desperately I want to.

However, his fingers toy with a tiny hole in the lace side until it widens, then a snap of freedom relieves the pressure of the band around my waist and inner thighs. Logan sinuously slides the ruined panties through my soaked cleft before stuffing them in his back pocket, a wicked grin brightening his otherwise harsh expression.

"You ripped my panties," I say dumbly, shock and exhilaration pumping in my veins.

"They were in my way." He proves his point by diving forward again, and this time the rough lap of his tongue on my clit singes every nerve from head to toe.

He wastes no time sucking on the sensitive bud as his calloused palms knead my ass, urging me closer for his possession.

Dim light flashes across my face, and I catch a glimpse of tussling men through a peephole in the stacked punching bags blocking our actions from view. It occurs to me that anyone could peek in from the other side to witness Logan on his knees, his head buried between my thighs—the obvious position indicative of our illicit affair.

God, that shouldn't turn me on.

Tangling my hands in Logan's hair, a sense of euphoria overcomes me as I'm bombarded with pleasure.

His beard scrapes against my inner thighs and exposed pussy. His lips suck my clit with rhythmic pressure as two of his fingers sneak between my legs and plunge into my wet channel. The sensation of fullness has me arching deeper into his touch, yearning for more.

More rough grazes of his fingertips along my clenching walls.

More insistent licks of his tongue teasing my throbbing clit.

More of everything.

A hungry growl vibrates between our bodies and his talented mouth devours me while the thrusting of his fingers becomes harsher, until everything coalesces into a lightning bolt of pleasure.

"Logan!" The climax shatters my composure and leaves me weak-limbed, limp and shaky in the strong, protective hold Logan has on me.

Muscular arms wrap around my waist as he rises to his feet, and my head falls to his chest, finding comfort in his rapid heartbeat—a tell-tale sign he's as affected as I am.

"Shh... Little Owl, I've got you."

He murmurs quiet reassurances after wiping his gleaming mouth on his forearm while one hand carefully tries to readjust my clothing.

Finding purchase on his broad chest, I push far enough away to raise on my tiptoes and kiss the side of his neck, the only spot I can reach in this position.

"Thank you... That was... I don't know what..."

Logan nuzzles my cheek. "You don't have to say anything. It was my pleasure, believe me." We stand like that for a couple more minutes before he says, "I'll give you a ride home."

Flustered from my orgasm, I shuffle backward and shake my head, declining his offer. "I appreciate it, but Kat's actually picking me up. I texted for a ride before running into you. She might already be here."

Imagine if she's been outside all this time while I was enjoying my first experience with a man going down on me.

Kat would understand.

An amused chuckle stalls in my chest as I consider the possibility.

We emerge from behind the punching bag wall to see the fight still going full-swing, but Logan doesn't seem to care about it.

Obviously. You think he'd choose to eat you out if the fight concerned him?

"I hate leaving you for the night," he grouses, and I hide a smile at his disgruntled tone. "I'll walk you out, so you're not waiting alone if she's not here."

He stops to say something to Fox before we continue to the parking lot where Kat's gold Camry hasn't appeared yet.

A strange zen feeling washes over me, the aftermath of such high emotions from earlier, and I ask the one question I've held as a barrier between us.

"Are you a criminal?" Not as eloquent as I would've liked, but I'm not sure how else to ask what I want to know.

"What?" His brow furrows and he chuckles at the idea.

Embarrassed, I elaborate, "The Reaper's Wolves, your club, do you guys have illegal dealings?" Now, I sound like a freaking lawyer during a deposition. Did that orgasm completely fry my brain?

"Is that why you've been reluctant for anything to happen between us?"

"Partly."

Sighing, he drags a hand down his beard before tucking it in his front pocket. "We're legit. Just a brotherhood of veterans transitioning back into civilian life."

"I see." That wasn't what I expected him to say. "That's why you got involved?"

"My dad was the former president. It's my legacy, but it doesn't have to be for my own kids."

"You have children?" I ask, surprised.

"Not yet." The way he looks at me makes me think he's talking about our future, but that's impossible.

Isn't it?

"Oh."

"Does this change things for you?" His rough palm cups the back of my neck, his thumb stroking the tense muscles softly as I consider his question.

Looks like I don't have to worry about getting involved with a criminal. But is that enough?

"I don't know," I answer honestly.

He sighs and nods toward a bench a few feet away. "Until you do, you should probably wait over there for now."

My nose crinkles in confusion. "Why?"

"Because if you don't, I'm liable to hike you over my shoulder and steal you away on my bike before your friend ever arrives."

My eyes widen in shock, but I see how serious he is. And it's turning me on again.

Before I can test his resolve, headlights from Kat's car flash as she pulls up to the curb.

"Hey, girl! You alright?" Her gaze bounces between me and Logan, a million questions flying across her face.

This is gonna be a fun drive home.

Logan's still watching me like a starving lion, and he takes a warning step forward as if to follow through on his statement, which jolts me into action. Hurrying over to the car, I hop into the seat and buckle in, waving goodbye as we drive away.

"It's obvious things took a turn after you texted..." Kat drawls.

"Yes, they did, but can we talk about it later when we're all together? I'm tired."

Kat reaches over to squeeze my knee before placing it back on the steering wheel. "Alright... You rest. Just know you're not getting off this easy tomorrow."

Leaning my forehead against the window, I exhale a heavy breath.

What a night.

My first blind date transformed into an entirely different man eating me out amongst a sea of people. It's a lot to process and exhaustion weighs on me.

Sleep. I just need sleep.

I'm not ready to examine the emotions Logan stirs within me yet. And I'm definitely not ready to decide what our future will be.

So don't.

There's always tomorrow.

Nodding to myself, I drift in my zen state for the rest of the drive, content with the decision to wait.

CHAPTER FIFTEEN

CAROLINE

"How was your date? That was this weekend, right?" Lindy asks as she stops by my cubicle Monday morning. I take a sip of my coffee, wondering how to describe what happened Friday night.

Spinning around in my seat, I sigh and motion for her to pull up one of the guest chairs sitting in the lobby opposite my cube.

"That bad?" She drags a chair across the carpet and settles in. After I relay the night's events in a hushed tone, Lindy releases a low whistle. "Wow... That's... a lot."

"Tell me about it," I agree. An email pops up on my computer screen drawing my attention. "I can't believe how rude Tyler was. Forget about not being interested romantically. I'm still a person."

Deleting the spam, I turn back to her. "But enough about me. What's up with you?"

"I'm fine. My boyfriend Dean's fine. We're fine...." The litany sounds like a familiar one. As if she's repeated it multiple times to force herself to believe it's true. Pausing, her voice drops. "Actually, that's a lie."

"What do you mean?"

Lindy nibbles her bottom lip, her eyes panning back and forth between me and the open space outside my cubicle.

"Do you want to go on a walk? I don't really want to talk about this here." The words fall to a whisper as another one of our coworkers walks by, and I nod in agreement.

Five minutes later, we're outside the building following footsteps on the sidewalk. The building management team decided to paint different colored footprints outlining walking routes for their tenants to encourage us to exercise throughout the day. Especially since we're at our desks all the time.

It's a nice gesture and definitely a plus getting some fresh air during the day.

Lindy stares off into the distance before beginning. "So, I think you've noticed some bruising I've had before."

"Yeah, but I don't want to pressure you into something if you're not ready to share."

"I appreciate that." Lindy's arms wrap around her waist, hugging herself. "But I think I'm finally in a place to ask for help. I know we're not super close. We only work together. But I feel like I can trust you, and I don't have family around here. And because of Dean, I don't really have friends anymore either."

Abusive asshole.

"You don't have to explain. I'm here with whatever you need," I promise, matching my steps to hers.

"Thanks... I'm leaving him. That's the reason I need to talk to you." A trembling hand sifts through her hair before she stuffs her fists in her coat pockets. "I don't really have a support system around here. Thanks to Dean and myself for letting him..."

"No, don't blame yourself." I rub her shoulder in comfort as we wait for a woman to briskly pass us on the sidewalk. It's a dreary day full of clouds which, thankfully, means not as many people are out here as usual.

"I feel so stupid for not getting out before everything turned into this." A sheen of tears glazes over Lindy's eyes, but she stares up at the sky, rapidly blinking them away.

"Just tell me how I can help, and I'll be there for you."

"I don't know if I told you, but Dean's a cop."

Which will make it easier for him to find her with all of the resources at his fingertips.

"I don't plan on bringing my phone when I leave during his tour on Thursday. So, I was wondering if you'd mind buying a prepaid phone for me?" She pulls out a wad of cash and offers it, but I wave her off.

"Of course. And you don't need to pay me for it. Consider it a housewarming gift for wherever you end up." Buying a prepaid phone to help her out of a bad situation is the least I can do.

"Thank you..." A grateful smile tugs at the corner of her lips as her shoulders slump forward. "I'll pick it up from you Thursday, if that's okay? After work, I'll pop a couple of boxes in my car from the house, then I'll be gone."

"Do you know where you're going?" It's got to be terrifying fleeing your home with such haste. No time to properly pack your belongings. No guarantee of finding an affordable new place.

"Not really. I have money saved, and I hate burning it on a hotel. But that's what it's for. I don't really want to go to a shelter or anything. Although there's nothing wrong with those. I just... I don't know. Plus, Dean's sure to track me to a place like that."

Oddly, the Reaper's Wolves clubhouse comes to mind. If there's any place Lindy would be safe, it's there with all those burly guys trained in the art of defending people. They could definitely stand up to cops.

"What if I said I potentially know a safe place you can go?"

"I don't want to put you out..." she starts, and I shake my head.

"No, no. Not my place. Not that I wouldn't want you to stay with me, but I feel like it would be one of the first places Dean looks since we work together."

"You're right. What did you have in mind?"

"I'd have to check with the person." Easy enough since Logan's back to persistently messaging me.

He's apologized multiple times for not coming down to visit this weekend, but club business has kept him tied to Suitor's Crossing.

"If he says yes, then it would pretty much guarantee your safety, even from a cop."

"Jeez, who is this person?" Lindy stiffens in concern, her gaze narrowing.

"That's why I'm asking your permission first to even bring it up. Do you remember what I said about my date going badly? That was only half the truth. There's this guy I've run into a couple of times, and he was there, too. He's part of an MC club."

"MC... like a motorcycle club?"

"Yeah, he's the president of a club called the Reaper's Wolves, and they have this big warehouse for communal living.

The compound's full of ex-military guys, so I'm fairly certain you'll be safe there."

I hurry to reassure her when the color drains from her cheeks at the information.

"The ones I've met don't strike me as the kind to harm women, and I don't think Logan will refuse my request. But the question is do you think you would feel okay in such a place? I mean, it's a ton of men when you're trying to get away from an abusive one."

Lindy contemplates her answer in silence as we continue walking, our strides in sync and purposeful.

Finally, she says, "If it'll save me money so I have longer to figure out what my next move should be, I'll take it. At least I'll still have a job, since Jerry's letting me move to working remotely."

Way to go, Jerry!

Our boss can be a tough taskmaster, but it's encouraging to see this caring side of him.

"So you're okay with me asking Logan? They're a totally legit club. No drugs or anything illegal."

"Sure. Ask your MC president," she teases, relief loosening the tension around her shoulders.

I don't correct her with the whole Logan not being mine thing because at this point, he kind of is. I just have to decide what to do with him.

More like deciding what to let him *do to* you... *again.*

During lunch a few hours later, I call Logan from my car, requiring privacy for this conversation.

"Hey, sorry to be a bother, but I have a question for you," I begin once he picks up.

"You're never a bother, Little Owl. Shoot."

Tapping my hand against the steering wheel, the story spills out in a rush. "It's kind of a big favor. A co-worker friend needs a safe place to recuperate after leaving her abusive boyfriend. She's really nice and needs some form of protection around her, which is why I thought of you guys. The caveat is that her ex is a cop."

"Shit, of course he is." The derision in Logan's voice raises my hackles.

"What does that mean?"

"It means Everton's police force is a fucking joke. Ninety-percent of them are into some shady shit, so I'm not surprised one's beating on his girl."

"Wow..." *That's disheartening to hear.* "What do you think about letting Lindy stay at the clubhouse for a little bit? She has money saved, so I don't think she'll be there long. It's just a temporary solution while she figures out her next move."

"It's good if she stays here, but she doesn't have to stay at the clubhouse. We have some cabins on the property, so she can have some privacy."

I remember the cabins from the last time I was there and nod to myself. "Great, thank you so much, I really appreciate it! I'll let her know we're good to go. We're probably going to be there Thursday evening after we grab the last of her stuff."

"Do you need help?" he asks and his offer melts my heart even more.

Logan really is a good guy. How I ever thought he could be a legitimately bad guy dealing drugs or weapons is beyond me. Goes to show how wrong prejudices can be.

Just because a man wears leather and rides a Harley like Jax from *Sons of Anarchy* doesn't mean he's bad news.

"Nah, it's just some boxes. Shouldn't take more than five minutes."

"Okay, I'll be here. Then maybe you and I can talk after your friend's settled."

Butterflies wing to life in my belly at the seductive drop in his tone. "Right. I guess we should do that, huh?"

"And other things... if you're up for it," he teases, and my body tingles in anticipation.

Oh, I'm definitely ready for more. This thirty-one year old curvy girl is aching to have a certain sexy biker punch her V-card.

Logan's a solid man. Protective over those he considers his own like me and his club members.

Honestly, why can't my life be like a romance novel? Why can't I let the hot MC president claim me?

Because I'm scared I won't fit in? Because I'm scared he'll regret his decision?

None of that's guaranteed.

There's only one thing I know for certain—if I don't risk a relationship with Logan, then *I'll* be the one regretting my decision for the rest of my life.

CHAPTER SIXTEEN

CAROLINE

On Thursday, Lindy and I meet outside after work, and I pass a mini grocery bag to her. "Here's your new phone. I already programmed my number in there, and I texted you the address to the compound. We shouldn't have any issues with you following me but just in case."

"Thank you so much for this. I truly appreciate it." Lindy wraps me in a hug, and I squeeze her back firmly. The setting sun casts a warm glow across the parking lot, but soon it'll be dark, slowing our progress.

"It's no problem. Sorry I didn't step up to help or say anything earlier than this week."

"No, I don't blame you for anything. We're all good." Lindy unlocks her car and opens the door, nodding toward the street of traffic parallel to our office building. "Should we get going, then? Dean's working a double today, so we should have plenty of time to get my stuff out, despite the less than ideal timing with all this traffic."

The insurance money for my car replacement still hasn't arrived yet, so I'm stuck driving the economy rental the company's covering. Hopping into the compact car, I give Lindy a thumbs up from the driver's seat and follow her home, forced to go at a snail's pace for most of the journey.

When we finally park in her driveway, Lindy and I hurry inside to grab plastic bins of pictures and books along with a couple of black bags of clothing.

"I didn't buy any cardboard boxes because I was afraid he'd ask why I needed them," Lindy explains, hiking a bag over her shoulder.

"No worries, as long as you have everything you want."

Thirty minutes pass with us stuffing her SUV full, ensuring nothing of hers is left behind. Before locking the front door once we're done, Lindy takes apart her phone and smashes it to pieces with a mallet, then tosses them in the trash.

"I know he can't track it since I won't have it on me, but just in case I accidentally left a trail there, I don't want him to be able to..."

"You don't have to explain, it's fine."

"I can't believe I'm really doing this." Her hands are shaking as she tosses the mallet aside.

I wish I could comfort her more, but honestly she probably needs the relief of a safe space to realize she's okay rather than more words of encouragement.

Right as we separate to start the drive to Suitor's Crossing, flashing lights atop a black Charger whip into the front yard and an angry man launches out of the front seat. "What the hell is going on here, Lindy?"

"Oh shit, he's back early." Lindy's face goes ghost white as the trembling increases to full on shivers. "What... I thought you were working a double today."

"Chris is covering my tour because I had a feeling something was off. Guess I was right. What do you think you're doing?"

"L... leaving." She retreats baby step by baby step toward her car.

"The hell you are. Stop being dramatic and get your ass back in the house."

"No."

I'm proud of Lindy for standing her ground but the red pallor that comes over Dean's face is frightening. Almost like a bull about to charge and stomp a matador to death.

"What did you just tell me?"

"It's over." Her fingers tighten around the ring of keys in her hand, the jagged edges poking out from between her knuckles. "I'm leaving. Please don't make a scene."

"*Me* not make a scene? You're the one who's out here for all our neighbors to see, car packed up like a thief in the night. I'm not the one making a scene, Lindy. You are."

Dean advances, and as scared as I am, I block his path. "That's not true."

"And who are you?" He pauses to look me up and down, sneering at my obvious disadvantage to his six foot height.

"A friend. Lindy has every right to leave, so please just let her go."

"Why don't you stay the hell out of this?" he snarls, body charging forward again. "This is between me and my girlfriend."

Ignoring him, I order Lindy to get in her car. My focus remains on Dean, matching his moves to maintain a barrier.

"What? I can't let you—"

"Yes, you can. Just go."

Thankfully, Dean didn't block her car in. His anger got the best of him with the whole "driving into the yard" thing rather than parking in the driveway like a smart person would do.

Thank goodness for small mercies.

I hear Lindy's shuffling footsteps behind me, and Dean lunges forward.

"No, leave her alone!"

We're toe to toe now. This close I can see the flaring of his nostrils, the wildness in his eyes.

"You need to back off, bitch. This doesn't concern you." He grabs my arm with a bruising hold, but I don't make a sound, afraid if Lindy thought I was in danger she wouldn't go and then things would get a hundred times worse.

"Let me go."

"Looks like someone needs to teach you a lesson." He shoves me to the ground then races towards Lindy, but I lunge for his ankles and trip him up.

Dean slams into the grass as I hear a car door shut and an engine start. Tires squeal out of the drive and a breath of relief leaves me when the tail end of Lindy's car disappears down the street.

My relief is short-lived, though, when Dean's hands dig into my hair to pull my head up for a backhand to my cheek.

"Where is she going?" he demands.

Spitting out a mouthful of blood, I hold back tears of pain, unwilling to give him the satisfaction. "I don't know," I lie. "But I'm definitely pressing charges for assault."

"You won't get very far," he smirks, his grip tightening in my hair. "You're on private property and touched me first. But you have the right idea calling the cops. I have a few friends who can take care of you and Lindy."

Driving my nails into his harsh grip, I stumble to my feet, snag my fallen glasses, and take off on a jerky run to my car after he rears back in pain. His heavy breathing pants behind me, and fear like I've never known before pumps into my heart.

This must be how Lindy felt every single day with him.

I can't imagine what she's been through, because even this is scaring me to the point where I'm sure I'll have nightmares for the foreseeable future.

Shoving the key into the ignition, my foot lays into the gas, sending the car rocketing down the street away from Dean. I'm afraid he's going to follow me, but for whatever reason, he doesn't.

Though I doubt it's the last I've seen of him. He doesn't seem the type to make threats lightly.

I drive around aimlessly for who knows how long, afraid he's put out an APB to his friends. I don't want to lead him to Lindy, but I also don't want to go home. In the end, back roads lead me to Suitor's Crossing and the Reaper's Wolves compound.

Lindy's already there, and a couple of guys are helping her unload the SUV into a cabin close to the clubhouse. I'm glad Logan didn't completely seclude her from everyone. If anything were to happen, she's only a quick shout for help away.

Pulling in next to Lindy's SUV, I turn off the car and sit there in a daze. My head is throbbing from where Dean tore at my hair and slapped me.

Wouldn't it be something if I have another concussion? Gone my whole life without them then two within weeks of each other.

Hysterical laughter bubbles up as I gingerly rest the back of my head against the car seat. I don't want to get out. Honestly, I don't even know that I can stand without shaking like a leaf.

It took all of my adrenaline just to get me here safely. It probably wasn't safe to drive either because I barely remember the ride.

Logan approaches the car and knocks on my window, motioning for me to open the door. This *would* be the first time he sees me after the MMA fight, beat up and bruised.

Sighing, I pull the keys out of the ignition, grab my purse and step out—wondering what his reaction will be to the puffiness of my face from Dean's hit and my crying.

"What the fuck happened to you?" The rumbled words are dangerously quiet as Logan gently caresses a finger down my cheek.

Inhaling a breath, an explanation clogs my throat. Swallowing hard, I try to speak again, but nothing comes out. I stand there gaping like a fish out of water until Lindy runs over, tears welling in her eyes.

"Oh my gosh, what did he do to you? I'm so sorry! This is all my fault. I never should've left you!"

"This was your ex-boyfriend's doing?" Logan growls. She looks between the two of us, then nods.

"Caroline told me to run while she distracted him. I never would have left if I'd..."

"No, d... don't blame yourself," I stutter. "It was you he really wanted. Who knows what he would have done if he'd gotten to you."

"I'm gonna fucking kill him," Logan says, and a couple of agreeing grumbles surround us as the guys who'd been helping Lindy join the conversation.

It's Fox and Timber, the men I met before, and I can only imagine the damage they could do to someone like Lindy's ex.

"It wouldn't be smart. He's a cop, remember?"

"Yeah, and he can't get away with hurting you or your friend. We don't tolerate that shit around here."

Swaying on my feet, I brace a hand on Logan's sturdy chest. "I don't want to risk him knowing where Lindy is. If you get involved, it'll draw his attention."

"You think we don't know how to perform a covert mission, Little Owl? We're former military. Army, Navy SEALs, marines. Covert's in our blood. Don't worry about that bastard finding your friend."

"What if he arrests you, or his friends do? He already mentioned getting his friends involved..." I stop. Considering how upset Logan is, he doesn't need to know that I was threatened with more action.

"Did he now? Lucky for him I've got friends, too." Logan bends to scoop me into his arms, and I swiftly hang onto his shoulders after the abrupt movement.

I'm in no condition to feel anything other than fear, but with his strength surrounding me, a sense of safety sweeps forward.

"This isn't over, but that bruise and cut need to be checked. Saber can look you over, make sure you're alright."

Lindy follows us inside along with Timber and Fox.

"Saber!"

The familiar doctor appears, takes one look at my bruised face, and shakes his head before turning around and grabbing his stuff.

"Again?" he asks five minutes later as he gently swabs at the dried blood on my chin. "You can't keep making a habit of this."

"Trust me, I don't plan on it." I'm resting in Logan's lap, which would normally embarrass me—being on display for so many people—but his protective embrace calms my nerves.

"The good news is you don't have a concussion this time," he confirms, and I breathe a sigh of relief, considering I drove over an hour to get here.

"There's not much I can do for the split lip. It should heal on its own. Otherwise, let's get you an ice pack for your cheek, although we probably missed the window to reduce swelling."

"Thank you, Saber," I say, wishing I knew his real name.

Holding the ice pack to my face ten minutes later, my head rests on Logan's shoulder in the communal living room as he pelts Lindy with question after question about her ex.

I'd warn him to stop, she's been through enough, but I don't have the energy to deal with another overbearing man today.

Not that Logan really resembles Dean, but it's still a lot of testosterone for one day. When he's gotten what he needs from Lindy, he orders Fox who'd been listening in to start making some phone calls, and Lindy checks in on me again.

"Are you sure you're alright? I'm so sorry."

"I'm fine. I should have expected something after stepping in between the two of you. I'm just glad you were able to get away. That's the most important thing."

"But I hate that you were collateral damage."

"Small potatoes in the grand scheme of things, Lindy. It's you he wanted but couldn't get. You can relax in Suitor's Crossing, which from what I've seen is a super cute town, and I'm kind of jealous that you get to live here."

"Well, it doesn't have to be just me," she says.

She's kidding, although there's a note of hopeful sincerity in her voice, and it makes me contemplate my future. Logan must approve of the subtle suggestion, too, because his hold on me tightens.

Everton's not my hometown or anything. I moved there for my job, which now has the capability of being remote. My book club girls are there, but it's not a terribly long trip to Suitor's Crossing. We could still meet up and Lindy could join us, since it's obvious she needs a support system.

Lindy mistakes my silence for disapproval. "Sorry, I shouldn't have mentioned something like that. Just because I have to uproot my life doesn't mean I should ask you to do the same."

"No. I don't mind that you asked. And I don't hate the idea. Suitor's Crossing is more my speed with the small town feel and the mountains literally in your backyard. Plus, you could use somebody to go in on an apartment with," I assume.

"That obvious, huh?" She blushes in embarrassment.

"It's nothing to be ashamed of. Rent these days is through the roof."

"Though I'm not planning on kicking you out anytime soon," Logan interjects with a pointed stare, and I squeeze his hand in silent gratitude.

"But I can't ask you to break your own lease and leave your friends and everything." Lindy shrugs, her chin tucking into her chest. " I don't want to be a charity case. Just forget I said anything."

"I'm not going to forget it. I'm going to think about it. It's a big move, and I'll have to talk to our boss about me moving remote, too. Not sure how he's going to feel about two of his employees skipping out on the office at the same time."

"Considering how vital we are to the company, I'd say he better get on board if he wants to keep us." Lindy laughs.

"Agreed. And I wouldn't mind having you closer either..." Logan kisses my temple before asking, "Are you staying the night?"

"No, I have to drive home. It's getting late, and I just want to sink into my own bed." Though Logan's is tempting, I don't think I'm emotionally ready for that after the day I've had.

"I'll drive you," he says, helping me off his lap as we both stand.

"Oh, that's not necessary."

"I'm driving you. You're still recovering, and it would make me feel better knowing you got home safely."

"I guess it's your time wasted." If he wants to drive an hour to Everton and an hour back, who am I to stop him?

"It's not time wasted, baby. It's time well spent. Timber will follow behind us, so I have a ride home."

Warmth floods my body at his assertion. It's a small thing, but I like that he's determined to make sure I'm safe. That I'm worth a long drive. I'm not used to people going out of their way for me, but I could definitely adjust to Logan looking after me.

Nodding in acceptance, I hug Lindy goodbye one last time, although I'm sure I'll be back over the weekend. Logan and I meet up with Timber who's waiting by a truck outside, and I give Logan the keys to my car then settle in for a quiet drive.

A warm hand engulfs my own as we turn onto the interstate. It grounds me. Melts my heart like a cherry popsicle under the summer sun. I've never had someone so determined to protect me—never had a person like Logan in my life.

Then let him in, finally, dammit!

I've got to stop throwing up walls between us. Need to trust he has my best interests at heart.

Logan doesn't need me preemptively assuming things and making decisions based on those assumptions. Because it's only hurting us.

I see that now.

And I'm tired of hurting. Tired of being alone.

I want my protective biker. An army veteran. An MC president. I want all of him, and it feels good to finally admit it without shame.

CHAPTER SEVENTEEN

SNOW

"What the fuck?" I park on the side of the road across from Caroline's apartment. Two cop cars sit in front of her door as four men loiter around the hood of their cars, their lights flashing.

I don't like the look of this.

"What is it?" Caroline opens her eyes from where she'd been resting against the window and a gasp of horror fills the car when she recognizes one of the cops. "Oh my gosh, that's Dean. He must be here to follow through on his threat."

"Not if I have anything to say about it." I get out of the truck and slam the door, circling to stand in front of Caroline after she gets out to create a protective barrier between her and the men.

"Caroline Bowman, you're under arrest for assault against an officer. Hands behind your back." An officer approaches, a gleam of satisfaction in his dark eyes. "Sir, I'm gonna need you to stand aside."

"Like hell."

"Logan, do as he says or else they might charge you with obstruction of justice." Caroline's hand wraps around my arm as she gently tries to push me out of the way, but I'm not moving.

"This is bullshit. She didn't do anything wrong. He's the one who harmed her! Can't you see the fucking bruise on her face?"

That motherfucker Dean laughs. I've seen his picture after looking him up because of Lindy, and the smugness on his face makes my fist itch. I want to punch it away.

"Who's this? Come back with reinforcements after assaulting me?"

"It's the other way around."

I'm impressed Caroline's voice remains steady. I know she's not one for confrontation, and it's got to be against her urge to follow authority to speak up against a cop.

"We'll let a judge decide. Hanson, cuff her."

Another man nears, repeating the charges and waving his handcuffs in the air.

"You're not taking her," I warn. Timber is in the corner of my eye, watching from the side, waiting for my next move, and I know he's got my back.

The two of us can take these four guys down, no problem. It would cause more trouble, but I can't let them take my woman.

"Logan, it's fine. You don't need to get involved," Caroline pleads for me to listen. "I'll be out soon. I have the evidence on my cheek of what he did."

Turning to face her but keeping the guys in my side vision, I murmur, "Maybe, but they're not playing fair. Who knows what'll happen once they get you alone."

I don't want to scare her, but the thought of Caroline by herself with these guys scares the hell out of me. Best to warn her so she's somewhat prepared.

"I've got to trust that there's somebody good in their department. We can't just stand out here causing a scene and have them call for help."

"Listen to the girl," Hanson says. "Are we gonna have a problem here or you gonna come with us like a good girl?"

I growl at the term. No one calls her anything like that but me.

Caroline presents her wrists and the metal slaps across the pale skin causing her to wince. They Mirandize her and lead her to one of the cop cars, Dean chuckling at my obvious disgruntlement and his apparent victory.

They reverse out of the parking lot five minutes later, leaving me and Timber alone.

"What are you gonna do, Prez?"

"I'm gonna get my girl out," I promise. Dean's not the only one with contacts, so I need to see where Fox is with those calls I ordered him to make. We need to speed up the process to get my Little Owl free.

"You can head back to the clubhouse. I won't be returning to Suitor's Crossing until Caroline's with me."

"Nah, you stay, I stay. You're gonna need some backup."

A half-grin forms as my palm slaps his shoulder. "Thanks, brother. I got Caroline's keys, so I guess we can wait in her apartment until we get this sorted. At least I can pack her a bag."

"She's coming to stay with us?"

"Hell, yes. It's obvious she and Lindy aren't safe here."

Timber's brows lower at the mention of the abused woman in one of our empty cabins. "You're right. We've got to make that motherfucker pay for what he's done."

Damn straight.

The late night fades into morning as I work with Ollie to dig up some dirt on Dean. The bastard's not very smart because it wasn't very hard to follow his shady trails.

Which hopefully ensures our meeting this morning goes quickly and without a word of trouble from him.

"Let's cut to the chase," I say, after tossing a manila folder onto the hood of his car, crossing my arms and nodding. "Take a look."

We're meeting in an empty parking lot at the edge of town. Timber's hidden somewhere in case Dean decided to bring friends, but thankfully, it's just the two of us.

"What's this?" He flips open the folder and pulls out pictures and documents of his illegal dealings.

"It's a warning. Drop the charges against Caroline, then leave her and Lindy alone. Forget they even exist. Or else I'll share this with your superior. And I'm not talking about Deputy Colson. I'm talking about the man above him, who's not in your little boys' club."

Dean's jaw tightens, his fingers flexing around the paper. "You're blackmailing me? You know this is illegal, right?"

"There's a lot of illegal shit going down, Dean. In that folder. In this conversation. Just depends on what you're willing to live with."

"This is fucking bullshit. All this over two women." He slaps the folder against his thigh in anger, and I grin at his obvious discomfort.

Good. He deserves to squirm. Who knows how Caroline's feeling behind bars right now? And it's all because of him.

"You're the one who started this. You wanted to play games with Caroline, and now I'm proving she's not an easy target. She's got me and my entire club at her back. So does Lindy. Keep that in mind the next time you want to fuck around and hurt my girl. Got it?"

Dean glares, but nods before making a call to the precinct to release Caroline. Satisfied, I hop into my truck and drive out, thankful this piece of work is done.

Caroline will be free soon, and I'll be right there to pick her up and take her home.

My home.

"BELIEVE IT OR NOT, my life used to be boring."

"Did it now?"

Caroline's finally settled into my room after I picked her up outside the precinct. She spent thirteen hours behind bars and that's thirteen hours too many.

"Yep, I read four MC books before we decided to go to that bar on the fifth release. And ever since then it's been one thing after another."

"You're gonna blame the books?" I ask, reining in a chuckle of amusement.

"No, I'm gonna blame Kat for taking us to that bar," she retorts, brushing her wet hair from the shower she took to wash away the jail cell grime. "It's just strange how life works. You go years without anything interesting happening, then bam! A million things happen within the span of weeks."

"Sounds like the military. We had lulls of training and the next thing you know you're called out for a mission—praying it doesn't go to hell in a handbasket."

"How long were you in the army?"

"Eight years. I got out when my best friend Austin did. Although his was a medical discharge."

She pauses her brushing to ask, "Is he okay?"

"Yeah, he's fine. He had a lot of surgeries and hospital visits but he's doing alright now. He owns a bar in Suitor's Crossing called the Ole Aces and just got married. Luna's a great girl. Opposite of Austin, but they work."

Caroline shoves her brush back into the suitcase I packed from her apartment and crawls into the bed like it's something she does every night. Hopefully, it becomes a regular thing.

"Was it *heart sparks*?" she teases.

"You've heard of the myth?"

"Kinda hard to miss when there are signs everywhere. Then I googled the town."

Laughing, I nod. "Yeah, they claim it's *heart sparks*, and it *did* happen pretty fast."

"They claim? Does that mean you don't believe in soulmates and all that?"

"If you would have asked me a few weeks ago, I would have voiced my doubts, but now I'm not so sure," I admit, staring at her with intense purpose.

Caroline's my *heart spark*. I accepted the fact a while ago, but it's a lot to lay on her when she's just now giving us a chance.

"Oh?"

"Yeah, *oh*... Why don't you get some sleep? You've had a harrowing day." Best not to dive into the deep end too soon. Let her rest and recuperate first.

"As I always do before I end up here."

"Let's hope we change that pattern."

"Fingers crossed..." Caroline removes her glasses and sets them on the night table before drawing her knees to her chest. "Logan?"

The mood in the room shifts as she stares up at me in contemplation. Sitting on the edge of the mattress, I cover her hand with mine. "Yeah, baby?"

"Make me yours. Completely."

CHAPTER EIGHTEEN

CAROLINE

Logan's gaze narrows as he licks his lips. I've shocked him with my request, but if I'm going all in with him, that means giving myself freely to him in all ways—including in bed.

"Are you asking me to fuck you, Little Owl?"

"Yes, please... If I've learned anything in the past twenty-four hours, it's that you never know what can happen. Happiness isn't guaranteed." I shrug my shoulders. "Lindy's a good person, but she ended up with Dean, despite him being a cop—a job where he's supposed to be upstanding and protective."

Shuffling to my knees, I brace my hands on his shoulders and stare into his silver eyes, needing him to understand this monumental change within me. "But he isn't any of those things. Which made me realize bad men can be anyone. Because of who they are, not what they look like or what job they have." My heart pounds in anticipation as I finally admit aloud, "You're a good man, Logan Snow, and I want you to be my first."

"I'll be your only," he promises.

"My only," I repeat, smiling at the possessive tone in his voice. "So, are you going to join me in this bed or not?"

123

Logan whips his shirt over his head, and this time I don't turn away from the sight of all his glorious strength. He's a big guy with a hairy chest and tattoos covering his tanned skin.

He's all man, and he's all mine.

Though when Logan removes his jeans, I get a little more nervous based on the size of his erection stretching the boxer briefs.

"I'm gonna love you so good, baby," he says crawling over my body until we're chest to chest, his face hovering above mine.

"I'm counting on it," I tease.

Logan dips his head to kiss me, and I moan at his hungry fervor. Never in my wildest dreams did I imagine a man would want me as desperately as Logan does. Frankly, I didn't think I could elicit such a reaction with my short stature, chubby curves, and quiet demeanor.

It all adds up to someone who doesn't want to be in the spotlight, but with Logan, I don't mind being the center of his attention because he makes me feel seen. Makes me feel good.

His rough palm slides under my shirt and quickly tugs it off, leaving me bare before him, in nothing but my panties, since I didn't bother putting on a bra for bed after my shower.

"Finally," he growls before nipping my breast with his teeth. The slight sting draws a gasp of shock, but he swiftly soothes it with his warm tongue circling the sensitive nipple before switching to my other breast.

"I've been waiting to suckle these sweet tits for weeks." His fingers dip under my panties to stroke between my wet folds, the dual sensation of his mouth and hands bringing my arousal to an immediate precipice.

"Come on, baby," he orders. "Give me a quick one just to tide me over."

My body obeys because, apparently, I can't deny him anything, and an orgasm crests to completion as I shiver under his body.

Logan shifts further south and plunges his tongue into my clenching opening, groaning at the squeeze of my tight muscles. "Fuck, you taste good. I've missed this. It's been too long since I've had my mouth on you."

If I could speak right now, I would agree.

He teases my clit with his tongue before rising up and kicking off his boxer briefs, allowing his thick cock to spring free. It's larger than any of my toys at home, and my thighs clench in anticipation of the stretch of his body taking mine.

Claiming me.

"This virgin pussy ready for my big cock?" he asks, and I moan in response.

"Yes, please, Logan..." I plead. "I've been waiting thirty-one years for this moment." To lose my virginity, yes, but to also feel seen, desired, cared for by a man.

Because I know this is more than just sex.

No matter his MC lifestyle, a man who's only after his own satisfaction doesn't wait around as long as Logan has for me. Doesn't offer his own home as a refuge to my friend unless he's intending for more to be between us. Hell, he said I'd be his permanently at the MMA fight after eating me out.

"Don't make me wait any longer, Logan. Please..."

"Damn, you sound so good when you beg. I'm tempted to make you wait to draw this out for both of us. But damn if I can. I've been eager to feel the clasp of your pussy on my cock for weeks. We can go slow later."

"Yes," I pant. "Later."

Because this isn't a one and done sort of relationship.

Logan's hips rear back before thrusting forward and burying his cock deep. "Fuck," he says under his breath. His fingers clench on the bedspread beside me as my own hands grip his burly arms for purchase.

"I can't believe you've been saving this pussy for me all these years, baby. So goddamn sweet and tight. I'm never gonna wanna leave this room. Let alone run my club while knowing that I can be balls deep in this cunt."

His filthy words excite me. I love the feeling of demolishing his filter, of causing him to lose control.

Logan doesn't give me much time to adjust to him before launching into a rough pace, slamming forward to hit my G-spot again and again. My back bounces against the bed as I just accept the pounding of his cock filling me to the brim.

It's hard and raw.

Not the usual pace I set for myself.

But necessary in this instance, because all I want is to feel Logan coming inside me. Feel the moment he claims me as his for good.

His thumb lowers to circle my clit, and a high keening noise leaves my throat. Something I would normally be embarrassed about, but what can I do when he's making me feel so good?

His harsh thrusts maintain a heavy pace as his thumb and finger pinch my clit, his mouth moving to circle my nipple.

My lungs struggle to draw in a breath until the tension finally breaks.

A cataclysmic orgasm rips through my senses, shooting bright lights behind my eyes.

"Logan!"

He grunts in pleasure, his movements becoming unwieldy before his own climax takes over, the warmth of his release coating my walls before dripping down my thighs.

Good thing I'm on birth control.

Not because I specifically planned on having sex soon, but to help with my periods. Never thought I'd be happy to be on the pill, yet here we are.

Logan rolls over and takes me with him so I'm laying atop his chest, fighting to even my breathing.

"That was perfect..."

"Just like you," he finishes my sentence, tucking a sweaty strand of hair behind my ear. "And worth the wait?" he questions.

"Definitely."

We lay there in silence, both of us gathering our thoughts after such an intense moment, and I can't help but smile. I'm virginity free, finally.

And I lost it to the hot MC president. Something I never would have imagined that first night we went to No Man's Land.

Kat's gonna love this.

ON SUNDAY, THE BOOK club gathers in Lindy's new living room with our drinks. The girls were ready to besiege the compound Friday when I got out of jail, but I held them off until today. It helped that I teased them about Logan and let slip that my virginity was a thing of the past.

"Thanks again for hosting us," Amelie says, raising her glass in salute.

"No problem. When Caroline suggested having a girls' night here, I couldn't say no. It's been so long since I've had a group of girlfriends. It's nice to break the ice again."

"Well, I know we just met, but you can count on us. Caroline hasn't told us much of what's happened, but we get the gist and we're really proud of you for what you've done. And now our dear Caroline is an ex-criminal for her role in it." Kat winks from her place on the couch.

"Oh my gosh, no I'm not."

"You were arrested with handcuffs. You spent the day behind bars. Makes you a criminal in my book."

"A falsely accused one," I point out. Those hours locked in a jail cell had been enlightening to say the least. Two other women were with me, though they kept to themselves, thankfully.

The irony wasn't lost on me how I'd feared hanging around Logan due to his ties to an MC when it was dirty cops I should've worried about the entire time. They were the ones to toss me in a cell—nothing relating to Logan and his crew.

"Whatever. It seems your biker president is rubbing off on you. Weren't you afraid he was a criminal, too?"

Is Kat a freaking mind reader?

"You were?" Lindy asks, eyes wide.

"Briefly, but he cleared that up," I reassure her. I never would've suggested she stay here if I didn't trust they were good guys. "They're just a club of veterans who follow the law."

"So, *you're* the bad influence, then." Kat's brows wiggle suggestively, and I roll my eyes. I'm never going to live this down with her. Though, I'm glad I can laugh about this now rather than remain paralyzed by fear.

Logan's done a lot to make me feel safe. *And adored. And downright sexy.* But those details are for me alone.

"Apparently. Can we move on to a different topic?"

"Sure," Amelie says. "Let's talk about the hottie that showed us to Lindy's house."

"Timber?"

"Yeah, that tall drink of water. I could climb him like a tree."

Beth chokes on her drink. She's been quietly listening to our banter from an overstuffed chair by the fireplace. "Oh god, please don't quote *Bridesmaids* right now."

Amelie, Kat, and I laugh because it's one of our favorite movies, and we quote it all the time. Beth used to love the film, too, until we ruined it for her with all the jokes.

"He escorted you to the cabin?" Lindy asks, a flush on her cheeks.

"Yeah, once we pulled in and parked at the clubhouse, he barreled out of the building like a man on a mission. Someone must have told him we were here to see you, Lindy. He kind of looked like he was about to protect your honor or something. Maybe he has a crush on you?"

"Let's hope not. I'm staying far away from relationships for a while."

"Good luck with that with all the hot guys walking around out here. I swear, you two got your men. It's time to hook a friend up," Kat declares, staring pointedly at me.

I shrug, sinking further into the leather sofa. "I don't know anyone well enough to make a recommendation. Saber is handy for scrapes. Fox seems full of charm. That leaves Timber and Logan—or Snow, to you all—and we've just decided they're taken."

Amelie taps a finger to her mouth. "I don't mind a doctor. Means he's good with his hands."

"Oh, look at you!" Kat playfully bumps her shoulder against Amelie's. "Being all logical about the choice."

The conversation continues from there with fits of giggles erupting every so often because of Kat and her ridiculous comments. It feels good to be with my friends again.

So much has happened this weekend, but this feels normal. Right. Like maybe my life *can* withstand the intense MC world mixing with the routine of my every day. I've already decided to go all in with Logan, that isn't going to change.

But this glimpse into how our future could play out—me spending time with him at his compound then hanging with my girls—fills me with happiness.

CHAPTER NINETEEN

SNOW

With Caroline safely ensconced with her friends at Lindy's cabin, I've only got one more thing left to do this weekend. Ollie found the rat in our club, and it's time to make him pay for what he's done.

Timber and Fox already have Snake waiting in our club meeting room while the rest of our men wait for my arrival.

"We all know why we're here." I meet everyone's gaze and each man nods except for Snake, still pretending stupidity.

"Not sure I do, Prez."

"Really?" I motion to Ollie, who plays a recording of Snake's voice sharing the security codes with one of Breaker's men. "We know you're the mole in our group. The reason there have been multiple robberies at our businesses. What we don't understand is the reason why."

"Money, plain and simple." He shrugs, flicking dirt from under his fingernails. "And a bit of fun."

A growl of anger rumbles from my chest. "Fun? You think fucking with our businesses, our livelihoods, is fun? All for an extra windfall in your bank account? What about your son, Alaska? Do you even care how this will affect him?"

Alaska's been up north on a fishing boat for the past six months, partially to avoid his father, Snake, but mostly for some quiet after getting out of the army. Their father-son relationship has never been easy, but this will probably break it into irreparable pieces.

Snake snickers. His amusement over the serious crime rankles everyone's nerves as men shift, cracking their knuckles or gritting their teeth.

"Y'all are brotherhood to the end. 'Oorah.' I don't give a fuck. Military life sucked, no matter how much you want to pretend it didn't. And Alaska? That boy doesn't give a shit about me. This is just me repaying the favor."

Disgusted with his logic, I ask, "Then why'd you even join?"

We don't force members into the MC. Men freely decide to patch in because we offer a brotherhood they miss from their time spent in the military. Snake's been a part of our club for years, joined back when my dad was president, which makes Alaska another legacy member like me.

"I don't owe you pissants an explanation. Thought we'd be making bank like the Ghost Rider MC by now. Instead, y'all act like a bunch of men when in reality you're nothing more than castrated sissies. Thought you might be smarter than your dad. Guess I was wrong."

His words are fuel to an already raging inferno. How dare he drag my dad into this?

"Are you fucking kidding me? You're gonna insult a room full of men who put their lives on the line for your sorry ass daily?" Repulsion balls into a knot in my stomach. "Remove his cut, and kick him out of here. You're gone."

Snake shrugs out of his leather cut denoting the Reaper's Wolves MC and tosses it on the floor before stomping out of the room, escorted by our enforcer.

"Good job figuring out who it was, Ollie." A couple of members pat him on the back for the solid detective work of sussing out the literal snake in our midst.

"No problem, Prez. Sorry it was one of us. Alaska ain't gonna like it." The rest of the guys nod. It always sucks when the betrayal's from your own side, but at least he's gone now. Our crew is secure again.

All I've gotta do is let Alaska know about his bastard of a father.

Fortunately, that can wait a little bit. He's bobbing about somewhere in the Bering Sea, unlikely to be able to receive a phone call right now.

Which means it's time for me to find my Little Owl and celebrate.

MY KNOCK ON THE CABIN door halts the ruckus of whatever's happening inside. Stumbling and hushed giggles ensue before Caroline opens the door, leaning heavily on the dark wood.

"Well, hello, Mr. President," she drawls.

Laughing at her Marilyn Monroe impersonation, I ask, "Are you drunk?"

"No, no, no. Just slightly tipsy." She puts two fingers close together.

"Well, I came to see if you were ready to go home." *Home* being my private cabin.

After that first night of her sleeping in my bed, I moved us to the cabin for privacy—not wanting to run into any of my guys or the women who hang out at the house.

Though, thankfully, I kicked Tiffany, the real troublemaker, out after that horrible night she broke into my home.

"Um..." She contemplates her answer while the girls behind her giggle and shout, "Yes, she's ready!" and push her towards me.

"Have fun, you two." Kat wiggles her fingers and winks, and I shake my head in amusement. That girl's wild.

Caroline and I walk the short distance to my cabin. As soon as we're inside, I shove her up against the door and drive my hands under the oversized sweatshirt she's wearing.

"Mmm..." she hums. "Are you about to fuck me against the door, Mr. President?"

"You're really feeling the title tonight, aren't you, baby?"

"What can I say, I like a man in uniform, a man with authority."

"Lucky for you, your man's got both."

"Yep," she pops her "P" and I grin. She's too fucking adorable for her own good.

Tossing her sweatshirt aside, I make quick work of the rest of her clothes until we're naked and I've hiked her into my arms, her legs wrapped around my waist.

"Hold on, baby, this is gonna be a wild ride."

"Promise?" she teases.

My answer is to line my cock up with her wet pussy and drive forward without preamble. That whole Mr. President shtick really must get her hot if she's this soaked from a walk from Lindy's cabin to here.

Bending towards her neck, my lips find my mark and suck hard, continuing to ensure it remains. Everyone needs to know she's my woman and I'm her man. Nothing's gonna change that.

"God, I love when you do that," she moans.

"This?" I circle my hips, grinding against her clit. "Or this?" My fingers pinch her nipples, tugging and rolling the sensitive flesh. "Or maybe this?" I suck harder on the delicate skin of her neck.

"Well, I love all of the above, but I really like wearing your mark. The girls make fun of me for it, but I think it's hot."

"It *is* hot because it means you're mine." I thrust higher, shoving her into the door, and her hands brace around my neck, tugging me close for a kiss.

"I'm glad I stopped being so stuck up and finally gave in to this."

"You weren't being stuck up, you were being cautious, which was smart. But I'm glad you've finally seen the light. I would never harm you. You're always safe with me and any one of my club members. We'd lay down our life for you."

"Don't say that. I don't want to think of any of you hurt."

"Just speaking the truth, baby. But, hopefully, it doesn't come to that," I agree. Slowing the pace, I secure her in my arms and walk us to the kitchen table and chair, sitting down with her in my lap. "Now, why don't you ride me, Little Owl? Ride your man."

And, fuck, does she—her body swaying atop mine, her curves bouncing, teasing me with their lush generosity. I could stare at her forever and never tire of the view.

My Little Owl is beautiful inside and out, which makes me the luckiest man around here.

Suitor's Crossing's *heart sparks* have struck me, descended on my life without preamble, and I couldn't be happier.

Because I adore my Little Owl, and I'm never letting her go.

EPILOGUE

CAROLINE

ONE MONTH LATER

Once things settled in our lives—Lindy was left alone by Dean and I got permission to work remotely—I moved to Suitor's Crossing.

Logan ended up telling Lindy she should just stay in her cabin instead of trying to find an apartment somewhere. At first, she refused, but once they worked out a cheap rent they were both okay with, she stayed, and I just moved into our cabin with Logan.

It's weird living on an MC compound, almost like college with so many people around, but it's not a bad weird. I actually kind of like not being alone so much.

It took some getting used to all the women around just to sleep with the guys, but most of them aren't terrible and I can't blame them for wanting a chance at one of the hot Reaper's Wolves members.

Former military mountain men, and they ride a motorcycle?

Can any woman be blamed for wanting a taste of that?

"What are you thinking about, baby?" Logan asks from across the table. We're waiting for his best friend Austin and his wife, Luna, to show up.

It'll be my first time meeting the couple, and I'm nervous.

"Just about how happy I am. How much things have changed in my life."

"For the better, I hope."

"Of course."

"I've been thinking I need to write a thank-you letter to the author of that book of yours. If it wasn't for her we may not have ever met."

"Her and Kat," I remind him.

"Hey, sorry we're late. We got held up by a train crossing Avenue E." A tall man and a woman with purple hair appear at our table, slipping into the empty seats.

"No worries. Austin, Luna, this is Caroline."

"Hi."

We all grin during the introductions, excited to finally meet, and I can't help but admire how cute of a couple Luna and Austin are.

They're quintessential "opposites attract" from what I can tell, with Austin in his dark jeans and navy henley while Luna is wearing a tulle skirt and a tucked in t-shirt with woodland creatures on it.

People stare at them, but I can't tell if it's because of their differences or because of the scars on Austin's face. Something Logan told me used to bother Austin more but doesn't now that he has Luna, which I think is really sweet.

It makes me happy that these two hardened veterans have found love in the world after living tough military lives. Whatever I can do to make my mountain MC president's life better I'm determined to do.

Fear doesn't hold me back any longer when it comes to him. I'm his "old lady," the woman who wears his name across her chest like he predicted—*Property of Snow.*

Because we're in love.

We're soulmates, *heart sparks,* and nothing will ever change that.

CHAPTER ONE

Faith

I'm silent—a church mouse trapped in a hell of my own making.

It wasn't supposed to be this way. The preacher's daughter caught in the crossfire between two rival motorcycle clubs, yet the lethal tension suffocating the room can't be ignored. Or escaped.

"We need to leave," Kelsey hisses from across the table. We're in a booth at the back of the bar, slightly separated from the stand-off occurring in the middle of the dance floor after a member of the Runners Ridge MC shoved a Ghost Rider.

Everything escalated quickly from there.

Is this what happens at the Ole Aces every night?

Known as a popular hangout for the Reaper's Wolves MC, a biker group who settled at the edge of Suitor's Crossing a few years ago, I've heard whispers of brawls breaking out over women and perceived insults.

My father's sermon that Sunday about resisting the devil's snare—as if riding a motorcycle and wearing leather condemned you to hell—echoes in my mind.

Just my luck that a mini vacation to Seattle would land me in the middle of another MC club's troubles. Who knew there were so many around?

"Faith? Come on. We need to sneak out before fists start flying and the cops show up."

Kelsey tugs on my arm to get me moving, but I'm stuck, riveted to the scene before me. I knew it was a bad idea to come here tonight. Or really any night.

Bars aren't my scene—nothing is as a preacher's kid.

But I wanted to take a risk, escape my protective bubble.

All my life I've followed the rules and been a good daughter—a good girl. I always consider how my actions will look to our church's congregation. How my words will reflect on my father. Especially after my mother died young, leaving me as her stand-in for matriarchal figure in the church.

It's exhausting and stressful, and I've been doing it for so long that sometimes I'm not even sure which part's an act and which is actually me. I wonder who I really am.

As a twenty-eight-year-old woman, it's not a good feeling questioning your identity, fearing you've wasted years of your life trying to appear perfect.

That's why I booked this getaway to Seattle. To experience a break from the judging eyes of High Ridge. It's a small mountain town full of kind people, or at least that's what I assume. However, most of my interactions are with our church's congregants, and they're... less than friendly, despite my stature as the preacher's daughter.

This weekend was supposed to give me a taste of freedom.

I was going to make a new friend in Kelsey, who I've been chatting with after connecting over Bumble's friend option, and broaden my horizons. Unfortunately, I wasn't expecting them to expand so far past my comfort zone that now we've ventured into a potential biker brawl.

I should've known when Kelsey suggested this place to meet that it was a bad omen. No Man's Land. It even sounds ominous.

But it also felt like my father was speaking and not me. So, I came.

Our table bumps into my belly as Kelsey abandons the booth in favor of the hall to our right leading to restrooms and presumably another exit. I tell myself to follow her—will my feet to move—but I can't.

I'm frozen.

A church mouse about to be swallowed whole as punches erupt amongst the shouting and all hell breaks loose.

Glass shatters as empty beer bottles slam across men's heads. Wood cracks under the force of chairs and tables being indiscriminately thrown. It's a madhouse of activity, and I can't tear my gaze away from the unfamiliar sight.

Never in my life have I seen men behaving so violently—rage pouring from their muscular bodies. The guys at church are always so respectful, in control of their actions. They don't fall prey to their "animal lusts" as my father would say.

At least not publicly.

Honestly, they're pretty boring, especially compared to these men.

A stray beer bottle whizzes by my ear before shattering on the wall, and I flinch at the close call. I've got to get out of here. If I return home with an injury, Dad will never let me leave High Ridge alone again.

Suddenly, a calloused palm appears in my line of vision and a gruff voice snaps the thrall the fight has on me—the deep tone far more intriguing.

"Come on, princess. I'm getting you out of here."

Don't miss Alaska and Faith's story in *Alaska's Lady*[1]!

THANKS FOR READING & DON'T FORGET TO RATE/ REVIEW!

Please consider leaving a rating/review. Ratings & reviews are the #1 way to support an indie author like me.
Also, don't miss out on free books and up-to-date release information. You can sign up for my newsletter here[1].
I appreciate your support!
XO, Hallie

---

1. https://www.thearrowedheart.com/hallie-bennett

ABOUT THE AUTHOR

Hallie prefers steamy, insta-love stories where curvy girls are claimed by filthy-talking heroes. And when she ran out of reading material, she decided to write her own stories. If you want a quick, hot read, she's your girl!

Printed in the USA
CPSIA information can be obtained
at www.ICGtesting.com
LVHW011736141023
761116LV00037B/695